Kalpana Chawla, the poet

On October 27, 1980 Kalpana Chawla wrote a poem to her friend, which she titled 'Toward the Goal'. The poem is reproduced as a tribute to brave astronaut.

Dive deep down

An aim awaits

Pearls peep

For your hands to reach

Just yours

For years, decades and ages

A door lies locked

A pearl in the shell

A secret in the brain

Open it

Break it

Reveal it

Fly high .

- Kalpna Chawla

INDEX

Chapter 1

KALPNA CHAWLA – BIRTH OF A LEGEND

A strong desire to travel beyond the blue yonder, to fly into the heavens and touch the stars some day... was all that Kalpana Chawla dreamt of.

Determined to the core Kalpana worked towards making her vision a reality. For this first female Indian-born NASA astronaut castles were not to be build on air but its foundation laid strong on earth.

Kalpna Chawla was one of the greatest astronaut ever born. She was a born astronaut and her only fantasy was to be an astronaut right from her childhood.

She became what she dreamt of & showed the world that dreams do come true with hard work & patience. She enlightened us with the way to success & showed us that one could achieve what one dreams with his strength, endurance, will power & confidence.

Chapter – 2

LAYING THE FOUNDATION

PERSONAL DATA: Kalpna Chawla born on 1st July 1961. Born in Karnal, India. She was survived by her husband. Kalpana Chawla enjoyed flying, hiking, back-packing, and reading. She held a Certificated Flight Instructor's license with airplane and glider ratings, Commercial Pilot's licenses for single- and multi-engine land and seaplanes, and Gliders, and instrument rating for airplanes. She enjoyed flying aerobatics and tail-wheel airplanes.

> *A strong desire to travel beyond the blue yonder, to fly into the heavens and touch the stars some day... was all that Kalpana Chawla dreamt of.*

Hailing from a traditional middleclass family, Kalpana was the youngest of the four children. Different from her peers even as a young girl, sketching and painting airplanes were more her forte than dressing up Barbie dolls.

Sanjay, her brother was her sole mentor throughout her journey as both of them shared the same dream and vision - to fly. Sanjay's plans of being a commercial pilot were shattered when his medical reports were not upto the mark. Kalpana went ahead to make her brothers and her own dreams come true and mind you it hasn't been smooth sailing.

Education:

Graduated from Tagore School, Karnal, India, in 1976. She got her bachelor of science degree in aeronautical engineering from Punjab

Engineering College, India, 1982. Master of science degree in aerospace engineering from University of Texas, 1984. Doctorate of philosophy in aerospace engineering from University of Colorado, 1988.

Academics and interests :

A brilliant academic record straight through school Kalpana took part in almost everything, from athletics to dance to science modeling. When she decided to join the Bachelor's Degree from Punjab University in Chandigarh, she happened to be the only girl in the aeronautics batch. Her family initial resisted her decision but they also knew that she was one determined woman and nothing could stop her.

Kalpana Chawla enjoyed flying aerobatics and tail-wheel airplanes, hiking, backpacking, and reading. She had a Certificated Flight Instructor's license with airplane and glider ratings, Commercial Pilot's licenses for single- and multi-engine land and seaplanes, and Gliders, and instrument rating for airplanes.

Career

At the age of 35 when most of the men are trying to build a career, her career graph had reached its peak. She was one among Rick D. Husband, William C. McCool, Michael P. Anderson, David M. Brown, Laurel B. Clark, Ilan Ramon (from Israel) the seven-member crew on Columbia which spent 16 days in orbit studying the effects of micro gravity on a variety of materials, focusing on how metal and crystals solidify when removed from the distorting effects of gravity....phew now doesn't that sound too complicated?

She was one of more than 2000 applicants for a civilian scientist's position on Columbia's voyage. According to NASA her academic accomplishments, intense physical fitness and experience as a pilot made her a natural choice. Carving her identity in an otherwise men's domain she comfortably shoulders her male colleagues.

Her second flight was a moment of joy for all Indians. Her return was eagerly awaited, but fate had other plans. When the space ship was just 16 minutes away from the earth, it exploded in the atmosphere. She will always be an inspiration to many young men and women as she has paved the way for them to dream. To think beyond horizons and reach for the stars...

Chapter - 3

NASA EXPERIENCE

AWARDS:

Posthumously awarded the Congressional Space Medal of Honor, the NASA Space Flight Medal, and the NASA Distinguished Service Medal.

EXPERIENCE:

In 1988, Kalpana Chawla started work at NASA Ames Research Center in the area of powered-lift computational fluid dynamics. Her research concentrated on simulation of complex air flows encountered around aircraft such as the Harrier in "ground-effect." Following completion of this project she supported research in mapping of flow solvers to parallel computers, and testing of these solvers by carrying out powered lift computations. In 1993 Kalpana Chawla joined Overset Methods Inc., Los Altos, California, as Vice President and Research Scientist to form a team with other researchers specializing in simulation of moving multiple body problems. She was responsible for development and implementation of efficient techniques to perform aerodynamic optimization. Results of various projects that Kalpana Chawla participated in are documented in technical conference papers and journals.

NASA EXPERIENCE:

Selected by NASA in December 1994, Kalpana Chawla reported to the Johnson Space Center in March 1995 as an astronaut candidate in the 15th Group of Astronauts. After completing a year of training and evaluation, she was assigned as crew representative to work technical issues for the Astronaut Office EVA/Robotics and Computer Branches. Her assignments included work on development of Robotic Situational Awareness Displays and testing space shuttle control software in the Shuttle Avionics Integration Laboratory. In November, 1996, Kalpana Chawla was assigned as mission specialist and prime robotic arm operator on STS-87. In January 1998, she was assigned as crew representative for shuttle and station flight crew equipment, and subsequently served as lead for Astronaut Office's Crew Systems and Habitability section. She flew on STS-87 (1997) and STS-107 (2003), logging 30 days, 14 hours and 54 minutes in space.

SPACE FLIGHT EXPERIENCE:

STS-87 *Columbia* (November 19 to December 5, 1997). STS-87 was the fourth U.S Microgravity Payload flight and focused on experiments designed to study how the weightless environment of space affects various physical processes, and on observations of the Sun's outer atmospheric layers. Two members of the crew performed an EVA (spacewalk) which featured the manual capture of a Spartan satellite, in addition to testing EVA tools and procedures for future Space Station assembly. STS-87 made 252 orbits of the Earth, traveling 6.5 million miles in 376 hours and 34 minutes.

STS-107 *Columbia* (January 16 to February 1, 2003). The 16-day flight was a dedicated science and research mission. Working 24 hours a day, in two alternating shifts, the crew successfully conducted approximately 80 experiments. The STS-107 mission ended abruptly on February 1, 2003 when Space Shuttle *Columbia* and her crew perished during entry, 16 minutes prior to scheduled landing.

Chapter - 4

SPACE RESEARCH AND YOU: STS-107 OVERVIEW

Most of the NASA experiments on STS-107 are sponsored by the Office of Biological and Physical Research (OBPR) and cover biology, physics, and chemistry. Other investigations will study different factors that control our terrestrial climate.

Fifteen investigations focus on the effects of space flight factors such as weightlessness on the functioning of basic body systems. Their subjects include a wide

Mission Specialist Kalpana Chawla scans paperwork for the STS-107 mission during training at Kennedy Space Center.

range of living organisms, including viruses, bacteria, fungi, rats and even the astronauts themselves. These studies will focus on changes due to space flight in the cardiovascular and musculoskeletal systems, in the systems which sense and respond to gravity, and in the capability of organisms to respond to stress and maintain normal function.

In biological applications, two separate Biological and Physical Research experiments will allow different types of cell cultures to grow together in weightlessness to enhance their development of enhanced genetic characteristics; one will combat prostate cancer, the other will improve crop yield. Another experiment will evaluate the commercial usefulness products from plants grown in space. A facility for forming protein crystals more purely and with fewer flaws than is possible on Earth may lead to structure-based drugs designed for specific diseases with fewer side effects. A commercially sponsored facility will house two experiments growing protein crystals. One will study possible therapies against factors that cause cancers to spread and a second for bone cancer which causes intense pain to its sufferers. A third experiment included in this facility will help develop a new technique of encapsulating anti-cancer drugs to improve their efficiency.

In a significant payload (another word for the experimental hardware or facility), a large, rugged chamber will host experiments in the physics of lean combustion, soot production and fire quenching. These should provide new insights into combustion and fire-suppression that cannot be provided on Earth. An experiment compressing granular materials will further our understanding of construction techniques that can provide stronger foundations for structures in areas where earthquakes, floods and landslides are common. Another experiment will evaluate the formation of zeolite crystals which can speed the chemical reactions that are the basis for chemical processes in refining, biomedical and other areas. Yet another will use pressurized liquid xenon to illuminate the behaviors of more complex fluids such as blood flowing through capillaries.

A single commercial payload carries more than 500 protein samples to be crystallized in continuing studies of the structure of life. Another commercially sponsored NASA payload is performing experiments involving a drug delivery technique. And after the flight, a NASA biospecimen-sharing plan will provide 36 types of tissue to 15 investigators (including three who also have in-flight studies) from NASA, the European Space Agency (ESA), the Canadian Space Agency (CSA) and the Japanese National Space Development Agency (NASDA).

The primary payload carrier on STS-107 is the new SPACEHAB research double module (RDM), doubling the volume available to, and significantly increasing the amount and complexity of, research that was possible on STS-95, the last such mission. The research double module is a pressurized environment carried in Columbia's payload bay and accessible to the crew while in orbit via a tunnel from the Shuttle's middeck. Together, the module and the middeck will accommodate most of the mission's payloads.

Of course, NASA is not the only space agency sponsoring scientific research on STS-107. ESA, through a contract with SPACEHAB, is flying an important payload focused on astronaut health, biological function and basic physical phenomena in space, the same phenomena that interest NASA is interested in, providing a more thorough description of space flight's effects, often in the same subjects or specimens. ESA will perform seven in-flight and one ground-based experiments on the cardiopulmonary changes occurring in astronauts. Additional ESA biological investigations will examine bone formation and maintenance, immune system functioning, connective tissue growth and repair, and bacterial and yeast cell responses to the stresses of space flight. A special facility will grow large, well-ordered protein and virus crystals expected to lead to improved drug designs. Another will study the physical characteristics of bubbles and droplets in the absence of the perturbations due to Earth's surface gravity environment.

SPACEHAB also makes it possible for universities, companies and other government agencies to do important research in space. The Canadian Space Agency is sponsoring three bone-growth experiments, and is collaborating with ESA on two. The German Space Agency will measure development of the gravity-sensing organs of fish in the absence of gravity's effects. One university is growing ultra-pure protein crystals for drug research. Another university is testing a navigation system for future satellites. The U.S. Air Force is conducting a communications experiment. Elementary school students in Australia, China, Israel, Japan, Liechtenstein and the United States are probing the effects of space flight on fish, spiders, ants, silkworms, bees and even inorganic crystals. STS-107 thus mirrors plans to have ISS foster international collaboration.

Columbia's payload bay also will house six science payloads making up the Fast Reaction Experiments Enabling Science, Technology, Applications and Research (FREESTAR) mounted on a bridge-like structure spanning the width of the payload bay. These investigations look outward to the Sun, downward at Earth's atmosphere, and inward into the physics of fluid phenomena, as well as testing technology for space communications.

While a conservative calculation puts the number of separate experiments on STS-107 at about 80, the mission comprises hundreds of samples and test points addressing dozens of facets of life on Earth. If even one eventually results in a new therapy - or cleaner engines, or some other benefit - then the investment the American taxpayer has made in STS-107 will be recouped many times over.

STS-107 thus continues a rich tradition of Shuttle-based life science, earth science, physical science and commercial research that is beginning to reap benefits in the new era of the International Space Station.

Chapter – 5

SELECTING RESEARCH

On the STS-107 mission, OBPR is NASA's lead science office and primary payload provider. NASA selected the life and microgravity sciences investigations for this mission with an emphasis on crew health and safety in preparation for extended orbital stays on the ISS. OBPR depends upon strategic plans from the National Research Council and the NASA Advisory Council as it develops its research goals and programs. Following this guidance and in support of long-term NASA objectives, OBPR solicits proposals from the internal and external research communities via NASA Research Announcements. An independent panel of experts evaluates submissions for scientific excellence. Ultimately, proposals are competitively selected based upon the convergent criteria of peer review scores, programmatic need, and funding availability. In the case of STS-107, scientific experiments were chosen from the queue of research that had already passed NASA's rigorous and competitive peer review process. OBPR-sponsored commercial research follows a separate selection process with commensurate emphasis on commercial investment, potential market and economic impact of product development using insights gained from space research, and viability. All OBPR selection processes are documented and available for review in accordance with ISO-9000 guidelines.

Busy studying in her residence hall room in 1984, Kalpana Chawla had no idea the pictures of space shuttles on her walls foreshadowed the path she would take.

The NASA astronaut and UTA alumna has orbited the campus from a larger perspective — space. She went in 1996 and is scheduled to go again in January.

"The only thing that strikes me now is I have pictures of my old dorm rooms, and in the rooms, there are lots of pictures of space shuttles," she said. "At the time, there was not a thought in my head (such as), 'Oh, this is the reason for putting these pictures up.' "

In fact, she said that convincing herself she planned this career from the start would be too much of a stretch. Her focus in college was learning about engineering.

"I really did find education very enjoyable," she said. "I enjoyed going to classes and doing the assignments and learning more in the aviation field."

Dr. Chawla enjoyed it so much that after receiving her bachelor's degree from Punjab Engineering College in India, she decided to continue her education despite receiving job offers.

"In my mind, after having done a bachelor's degree, I just didn't feel that I knew the subject as well as I ought to, and I really wanted to learn the basics far better," she said.

She said she chose UTA for graduate studies because of its teaching and research opportunities. She said adjusting to the new country and environment wasn't hard.

"University towns are similar everywhere because there are young students, and they interact with each other and carry on," she said. "Arlington being a university town, especially in aerospace, there are students from all over the world. It really didn't stand out from being different from what I had experienced before."

UTA stood out in her memory, she said, because it had a serious focus on teaching. Other universities she has visited often use teaching assistants in the classrooms instead of professors.

"For me, that part really stands out," she said. "Some really knowledgeable and experienced professors were teaching in the classroom, and, as a result, students benefited."

Don Wilson, mechanical and aerospace engineering chair and Chawla's UTA adviser, said that because of her attitude in the classroom, he was not surprised she became an astronaut.

"She was a bright, young, eager and enthusiastic student — a really talented individual," he said. "I figured she was going to be successful."

Aerospace Engineering Director Don Seath said he was pleasantly surprised to learn Chawla became an astronaut. "She was a very quiet person and a very good student," he said.

After completing her master's here in 1984, Chawla received her doctoral degree in engineering from the University of Colorado in 1988.

In 1996, she was the mission specialist aboard STS-87 and studied the effects of weightlessness in space.

The job of mission specialists, she said, includes assisting the commander and pilot, checking shuttle systems for problems and conducting on-board experiments.

But nothing could have prepared her for the launch, she said.

"During part of the launch ... it seems like someone three times your weight is sitting on your chest," she said. "As soon as the main engines cut off, it's zero gravity, and your hands, which were lying at your sides, come floating up. That's a very strong sensation because it's so suddenly going from having that weight on your chest to feeling free-floating."

The launch was only the start, she said. It couldn't compare to what she saw from the shuttle.

"Looking out the windows, the earth is really a breathtaking sight," she said. "As you come close to Australia and you see the (Great) Barrier Reef and how it shines with the sun's rays, it gives you an awe-inspiring sense that this planet is really very small."

Chawla is scheduled for launch again Jan. 16 aboard the STS-107 Spacehab.
Students who want to become astronauts can study in several technical fields, she said, but should make sure the field is so dear to their hearts that learning feels like fun.

"When you are going for a goal, the journey is the best part," she said. "If you don't even enjoy getting there, then most of the fun is out of it, and one should ask oneself if it's worth it."

Chapter - 6

MISSION COLUMBIA

CAPE CANAVERAL, Fla. -- Shuttle Columbia safely flew into Earth orbit Thursday, the start of a marathon 16-day mission in which seven astronauts will work around the clock in the name of science.

Israel's first spaceman, Ilan Ramon, was aboard NASA's oldest orbiter as the vehicle lifted off from the Kennedy Space Center right on time at 10:39 a.m. EST (1539 GMT).

Tens of thousands of spectators who had gathered along Florida's Space Coast amid tight security watched as the 18-story-tall shuttle cruised out over the Atlantic Ocean and climbed through clear skies toward space.

Concerned about potential terrorist acts in light of Israel's prominence on this flight, NASA and local authorities worked together to ensure the safety of those on and off the space center. No serious incidents or security breaches were reported.

Eight-and-a-half minutes after blast off Columbia's main engines were shut down and the external tank jettisoned. More than two years after they were selected for this flight, the crew flying NASA's oldest orbiter finally made it into space.

Originally targeted for launch in July 2001, the astronauts and scientists involved with STS-107 -- NASA's designation for the mission -- have had to endure lengthy schedule delays caused by fleet-grounding technical problems and higher priority shuttle flights.

But once the countdown finally began Sunday night, everything happened like clockwork. There were no technical problems and the weather cooperated.

"If there ever was a time to use the phrase all good things come to people who wait, this is the one time," launch director Mike Leinbach told the crew just before liftoff. "From the many, many people who put this mission together, good luck and Godspeed."

"We appreciate it, Mike," replied Columbia commander Rick Husband. "The Lord has blessed us with a beautiful day here, and we're going to have a great mission. We're ready to go."

Once in space, the crew were to immediately get to work, setting up the shuttle as an orbiting platform for science research.

Columbia's voyage -- the 28th flight for the orbiter and the 113th for the shuttle program -- is the first flight not going to the International Space Station since the same shuttle hosted a Hubble Space Telescope servicing mission in March 2002.

"This mission is fairly unique compared to the shuttle flights we've flown recently in that it is a dedicated science mission," said Kelly Beck, lead flight director for this mission. "It will span multiple disciplines, such as the life sciences, physical sciences, Earth and space sciences as well as the educational arena."

Altogether there are 86 payloads that will support 79 science experiments and investigations in the fields of biology, physical science, advanced technology and Earth and space sciences.

"We have a smorgasbord of experiments. There's no one principal focus with all of the payloads that we have on board," said Columbia pilot William McCool.

To fully take advantage of their resources in orbit, the crew will split into two shifts to work 24 hours a day.

Husband, Ramon and mission specialists Kalpana Chawla and Laurel Clark will be on the red team that works the day shift based on Houston time, while McCool and mission specialists Mike Anderson and David Brown will be on the blue team and work the overnight shift.

"We'll be very, very busy. This is a jam-packed 16 days on orbit," McCool said. "And if it were a jam-packed eight days on orbit, I just wouldn't have any time probably to look out the window. So, at least this way I get an opportunity to smell the smells, see the sights, write down some notes."

In addition to the seven humans, a menagerie of critters will be participating in the experiments including rats, fish, silkworms, spiders, ants and even some bees.

The studies deal with topics such as preventing kidney stones, improving construction techniques when building on sandy soil, how the ability to smell changes in space, as well as the usual assortment of shuttle experiments such as those involving crystal growth.

One experiment that is getting a lot of attention is the Mediterranean Israeli Dust Experiment (MEIDEX), which is the scientific reason why astronaut Ramon is flying this mission. Although he has trained to work on many of the other experiments, his main job will be to keep an eye out for dust storms on Earth.

The MEIDEX experiment involves pointing a special camera at the dust in the atmosphere and taking pictures, while at the same time aircraft will attempt to take measurements of the same area of the sky at the same time.

"Together with a lot of ground station measurements, the scientists are going to analyze this data after flight, post-flight, and try to better understand the impact of the dust on our global climate," Ramon said.

The MEIDEX hardware also will be used to look for a form of lightning called sprites -- statistically one sprite fires off above a thunderstorm somewhere in the world every second, Ramon said -- and to test the astronaut's ability to see specific objects on the ground at extreme slant angles.

Much of the work will be done inside a pressurized SpaceHab research module that is tucked inside Columbia's cargo bay and connected to the crew cabin by a tunnel. Also in the bay is a pallet of experiments called Freestar.

SpaceHab, Inc., built the Research Double Module being used for the first time on this flight and leased it to NASA. As part of the deal, the company sold 12 percent of the experiment space to commercial customers.

Columbia is to remain in orbit until Feb. 1, with a planned landing back at the Kennedy Space Center at 8:49 a.m. EST (1349 GMT).

Chapter - 7

ADVENTURES IN LOW EARTH ORBIT
- Deanna DeMarco & David Imboden

On November 19, 1997, Dr. Kalpana Chawla became the fourteenth astronaut with CU ties and the first Indian woman in space. She served as mission specialist on STS-87, traveling 6.5 million miles in 252 orbits of the earth aboard space shuttle Columbia. STS-87 was the fourth US Microgravity Payload (M.P.) flight and focused on experiments designed to study how the weightless environment of space affects physical processes. Two members of the crew performed two EVAs (Extra Vehicular Activity or spacewalk) featuring the manual capture of a Spartan satellite as well as testing EVA tools and procedures for future space station assembly.

The Interview

CEM: When did you first know that you wanted to be an astronaut?
KC: Actually, in my case I really wanted to fly. My dad used to take us for joy rides in small planes, and that was my first introduction to flight. In India, you took your major subjects early on. I was in 8th grade when I decided I wanted to be an engineer. In 11th grade, when you are 14, you had to determine which type of engineering and I declared aerospace. It just intrigued me and interested me even though my advisors tried to steer me into more popular engineering fields like mechanical or electrical.

My town had one of the 12 flying clubs in India so we were used to seeing the small planes flying, but I don't remember seeing one of the planes and saying, "Oh yeah, this is what I want to do." I wondered about taking lessons, but my dad didn't want me to. So I decided when I came to the US that I would fly, and that was when I started taking lessons.

CEM: You hold Certificated Flight Instructor's license and Commercial Pilot's licenses for single- and multi-engine land airplanes and single-engine seaplanes, instrument rating and Private Glider. How do you maintain all of these licenses?
KC: It's very expensive. I have a very cheap lifestyle in everything else. I hope NASA doesn't find out about the car I drive.

CEM: When did you decide you wanted to come to the US?
KC: In the back of my mind I knew that the US would have more airplanes than we would at home. It was very simple. It was so simple that I had my own definition of what a flight engineer would be. This person flew and fixed problems in the airplane while flying. When I got to engineering school I realized that a flight engineer doesn't fly, he just sits and navigates. [Deciding to come to the US] was more of a concept sort of thing: this is what I really want to do. In the meantime, I had fun [studying aerospace engineering]; it wasn't boring. I like to tell people that now because I know people who want to be astronauts who sort of suffer through their course work. I say that enjoying what you are doing now is the most important thing.

CEM: What was your area of interest in graduate school?
KC: It was aerodynamics. In Texas I studied the aerodynamic aspects of propulsion‹air flow through planes and through turbine engines. When I came to Colorado, I was first directed to work in combustion, but I really didn't enjoy it. I talked with Dr. Chow [her thesis advisor] if I could work with him, so I switched back into aerospace.

I enjoy aerodynamics even now. I feel starved for it in my current job. I have some of the old graduate and undergraduate level textbooks by my bedside that I open up and read and see if I still remember what a stream function is, things like that.

CEM: You only had to apply to the NASA astronaut program twice before you were accepted. What was the application process like and what in your background made you stand out?
KC: NASA advertises an opening for applications about every two years in local NASA journals and some trade journals. They seek particular fields, but I don't think that matters so much. You fill out the application and a committee goes through the applications and come up with a smaller group. They then ask for recommendation letters, have you do FAA medicals, and call you in for interviews.

The first time I did the FAA medicals, but I wasn't called for an interview. After the interviews, they do security checks, but you don't really know if you are in the final group until you are called.

A lot of people apply four or five times. My first grand chief had interviewed four times before he was selected. Some people progress farther in the application flow with every new application. So it is different for every person.

CEM: What was it like to get the call that you got accepted into the space program?
KC: The astronaut hopefuls maintain a network address and post everything related to getting selected there. I monitored some of their traffic to see if there was anything about when we were going to get called, but it wasn't very accurate.

When NASA did finally call, they used a very interesting line to let you know if you were selected: "We are wondering if you are still interested in coming down and working for the space program as an astronaut." [Who is going to say] "No, I don't think so"? I knew that this was the sort of language they would use, so I wanted to tell them then very professional, "Oh yes." But I do remember losing it for just a second.

CEM: What is NASA looking for in astronaut hopefuls?
KC: They are definitely looking for technical skills. Besides that, they look that you are a fully rounded person who does other things besides your work. I think they also look for your ability to talk to the group and get along with them in the interview. Beyond that it is everybody's guess.

CEM: What was training like? Are you required to move to Houston?
KC: Mine lasted fourteen months‹the length of training depends on the size of the class because you have to schedule simlength of training depends on the size of the class because you have to schedule simulator time.

You are required to stay in Houston. You work for the Space Program as an astronaut and space flight is part of your job. It's not the other way around. Every once in a while you are given a space flight and you train for that.

CEM: What are your day to day activities like when you aren't preparing for a flight?
KC: They are more technical engineering jobs. It is very dynamic. The projects are small and they need to get done and new things come up. I get cycled through different jobs every year. I could do robotics, work in the computers branch, or be a Cape Crusader. Cape Crusaders are the people at Houston who support launches at Kennedy, where you are involved with flight hardware. They are very different jobs and I enjoy that.

CEM: Moving on to the actual mission, what were your responsibilities during launch?
KC: The whole sequence is very fast. I was doing the photography [of the external tanks that contain the propellant and the oxidizer] and was very disoriented because I did not know where my legs

were. You only have two and a half minutes [to photograph tanks] because after that they are not going to be visible. During the time that it was in view I took about forty pictures. The people on ground were really happy because it showed them the sequence for how the venting was taking place-they hadn't seen it on previous flights. NASA did a lot of analysis to see if this small thing could become a big problem on another day and they concluded that it wasn't.

CEM: What experiments were you responsible for on this mission?
KC: I was responsible for all of the US M.P. experiments on our flight. The first day was very busy because everything needs to happen on time. For example, if you don't open the payload bay doors right away, the equipment will start to get hot. Likewise, for the experiments everything is plugged in on ground and is autonomous for the launch time plus whatever else it takes to get is started again. Once you are in orbit and using your fuel cells, you want to power the experiments up. We didn't have any surprises where everything started up okay.

CEM: There were a lot of different nationalities represented on your team. Was there ever a language barrier?

KC: Initially there was when were training because we had one member from the Ukraine [Leonid Kadenyuk] who didn't speak English very well. He took English lessons and improved so it wasn't a problem. Plus, we were all asked to take 80 hour Russian courses so we could speak a little bit of Russian. Not much, but enough so that if a word was too big for him you could open up your dictionary and show him what you were saying.

CEM: The Spartan deployment did not go exactly as planned. What happened?
KC: The first thing we did with Spartan was a status check after all of the commands had been given and everything was good. We deployed it and then it was supposed to do a pirouette, which it

didn't do. That tells us that it needed to be put back in the payload bay to do a reinitialization within one hour. We went to grapple it, but the attitude of Spartan is such that its solar inertia is supposed to look at the sun. The good thing is that if you deploy it you shouldn't have to come back, but if you do the camera is looking at this very shiny object. We couldn't make our cameras behave and there is nothing you can do. We kept going towards it, but the arm touched Spartan and, being very light, it started to spin. I backed off to try to grab it again, and the commander and the pilot flew the orbiter to try to match the rate Spartan was spinning, but we could never match the rate. But we were using up our allotted propellant for this experiment so we had to withdraw.

We knew we would have to do an EVA [spacewalk] to recover Spartan.

When NASA looked at it later to determine what went wrong. A lot of the problems were with the satellite and the software‹how could it give you a status check that was good when things weren't really good. They made a list of things that needed to be fixed before Spartan could be flown again. They also decided on things that were missing from our training. For example, we did not simulate those lighting conditions. Also, we don't have a established rules for how to match rates. Later it became apparent that we couldn't match that rate so we were just wasting propellant. The biggest thing against the crew was crew resource management where if more people had been watching what was going on, it could have been prevented. But then again, NASA said that there was no margin for error with the Spartan deployment.

CEM: Was there any concern about doing an EVA of NASA's oldest shuttle?
KC: No because an EVA had been planned for Columbia, it just hadn't happened. STS-80 was supposed to check out the space crane and the procedure for moving a battery from one location to another. But they had a problem opening the hatch so they didn't get to do it. One of the screws in the hatch mechanism had loosened and wedged itself, and there was nothing that the crew

could have done. So that EVA was then given to our mission.

CEM: Were you supposed to do two EVAs on your flight?
KC: No, it was supposed to be one. But we knew from our timeline that if we were going to fly Sprint we wouldn't have time to do it. In all of our training runs the tasks that we were supposed to do took longer than the timeline called for. We knew we wouldn't get an extension to fly Sprint because it had low priority. In the first EVA they spent the first couple of hours recovering Spartan and then they finished their primary tasks. When ground reviewed the trouble we had mounting the battery on the arm and the restraint system to control the vibrations when you put the battery on the arm, they wanted to make sure we could fly this thing on another flight. NASA decided to use the crew to check this thing with a few other ideas. The second EVA was designed from lessons learned on the first EVA. It wasn't leftover tasks that were delayed because of Spartan.

CEM: Looking at the daily reports from STS-87, NASA has the astronauts keep a rigorous schedule. How do you adjust to such unusual routines?
KC: You don't really adjust. Some people would have this constant one hour jet lag like they caught up to the previous day and now it is the new day. NASA does it for the planned landings. They want it to happen during daylight hours. They determine when the burn should happen and when the crew should be ready, it should happen during the early half of the crew's wake up hours. For this to happen there is sleep shifting throughout the whole flight by an hour or two hours to make sure that come landing day you can do a daytime landing.

CEM: Were you allowed to take any personal items on the shuttle? What did you take?
KC: You can take ten things representing groups you belong to. I took a CU medallion. [which she donated to the Aerospace Department during her visit to CU]. You can also take 20 CDs or

tapes. I didn't get to listen to them very much. I shared one with the crew during dinner "The English Patient Soundtrack". I also had classical Western and Indian music. I took twelve tapes and I only listened to three of them.

CEM: What was the most surprising or rewarding part of your whole space flight experience?
KC: Actually, I think it was the whole experience. In the big picture you can count a lot of the small things, but really it is the whole experience-including the training year. Like I said. it is important to me to work hard and have fun doing it. It was very stimulating. The earth view was just magnificent, but if that was the only thing it wouldn't be worthwhile.

The earth view is gorgeous. Just looking out is neat. You just hang-you can't feel your hands. It's not like on earth where you can feel the ground and your elbows feel the chair. The only thing I feel is my thoughts. There is nothing else touching me, telling me I have limbs. It's so natural, it's not anything special.

On the tenth or eleventh day, I wanted to do one full pass and sit by the door and watch the earth. Doing that was mind boggling. It really instilled this huge sense of how small earth is. An hour and a half and I could go around it. I could do all of the math and logic for why this was, but in the big picture the thing that stayed with me is this place is very small. I felt that every person needs to experience this because maybe we would take better care of this place. This planet below you is our campsite and you know of no other campground. I didn't think this view would be something so philosophical-I thought I would just go around and see the continents and the oceans, but it was much more than that.

Chapter - 8

DEATH IN THE FAMILY

On Saturday night, when news about the *Columbia* disaster reached a group of journalists partying at a resort in suburban Mumbai, there was shock, disbelief, and tears.

Moments later, the music was stilled as one editor called for silence to mourn Kalpana Chawla's death.

As the journalists gathered to watch CNN, some overcome by the images of the debris hurtling to earth left the room hurriedly. Others wept.

"She was a heroine," one usually cynical editor said, sadness sketched all over his face."It takes enormous ability to be an astronaut. You need to know a lot of everything, from biology to astrophysics to aeronautical engineering. In this era of super-specialisation, you have to be an encyclopaedist to be an astronaut. Her achievements are something to be in awe of."

That reaction was replicated in countless cities and towns across the breadth of the nation where Kalpana Chawla was born on Saturday night.

For millions of young Indians she was an inspirational figure, her story conveying so eloquently to them that they could dream and work hard to achieve their dream one day. The way she did when she dreamt of conquering the last frontier known to man, when she was at school in Karnal.

That frontier, which she chose to redefine by her initiative and scholarship, may have claimed her life on February 1, but Kalpana Chawla lives on for all eternity.

Chapter - 9

2003 SPACE SHUTTLE COLUMBIA
JOINT HEARING
BEFORE THE

SUBCOMMITTEE ON SPACE AND AERONAUTICS
COMMITTEE ON SCIENCE
HOUSE OF REPRESENTATIVES

AND THE

COMMITTEE ON COMMERCE, SCIENCE, AND
TRANSPORTATION
U.S. SENATE

ONE HUNDRED EIGHTH CONGRESS

FIRST SESSION

FEBRUARY 12, 2003

COMMITTEE ON SCIENCE

HON. SHERWOOD L. BOEHLERT, New York, *Chairman*

LAMAR S. SMITH, Texas
CURT WELDON, Pennsylvania
DANA ROHRABACHER, California
JOE BARTON, Texas
KEN CALVERT, California

NICK SMITH, Michigan
ROSCOE G. BARTLETT, Maryland
VERNON J. EHLERS, Michigan
GIL GUTKNECHT, Minnesota
GEORGE R. NETHERCUTT, JR., Washington
FRANK D. LUCAS, Oklahoma
JUDY BIGGERT, Illinois
WAYNE T. GILCHREST, Maryland
W. TODD AKIN, Missouri
TIMOTHY V. JOHNSON, Illinois
MELISSA A. HART, Pennsylvania
JOHN SULLIVAN, Oklahoma
J. RANDY FORBES, Virginia
PHIL GINGREY, Georgia
ROB BISHOP, Utah
MICHAEL C. BURGESS, Texas
JO BONNER, Alabama
TOM FEENEY, Florida
VACANCY

RALPH M. HALL, Texas
BART GORDON, Tennessee
JERRY F. COSTELLO, Illinois
EDDIE BERNICE JOHNSON, Texas
LYNN C. WOOLSEY, California
NICK LAMPSON, Texas
JOHN B. LARSON, Connecticut
MARK UDALL, Colorado
DAVID WU, Oregon
MICHAEL M. HONDA, California
CHRIS BELL, Texas
BRAD MILLER, North Carolina
LINCOLN DAVIS, Tennessee
SHEILA JACKSON LEE, Texas
ZOE LOFGREN, California
BRAD SHERMAN, California

BRIAN BAIRD, Washington
DENNIS MOORE, Kansas
ANTHONY D. WEINER, New York
JIM MATHESON, Utah
DENNIS A. CARDOZA, California
VACANCY
VACANCY
VACANCY

Subcommittee on Space and Aeronautics
DANA ROHRABACHER, California, *Chairman*
LAMAR S. SMITH, Texas
CURT WELDON, Pennsylvania
JOE BARTON, Texas
KEN CALVERT, California
ROSCOE G. BARTLETT, Maryland
GEORGE R. NETHERCUTT, JR., Washington
FRANK D. LUCAS, Oklahoma
JOHN SULLIVAN, Oklahoma
J. RANDY FORBES, Virginia
ROB BISHOP, Utah
MICHAEL BURGESS, Texas
JO BONNER, Alabama
TOM FEENEY, Florida
SHERWOOD L. BOEHLERT, New York

BART GORDON, Tennessee
JOHN B. LARSON, Connecticut
CHRIS BELL, Texas
NICK LAMPSON, Texas
MARK UDALL, Colorado
DAVID WU, Oregon
EDDIE BERNICE JOHNSON, Texas
SHEILA JACKSON LEE, Texas
BRAD SHERMAN, California
DENNIS MOORE, Kansas

ANTHONY D. WEINER, New York
VACANCY
RALPH M. HALL, Texas

BILL ADKINS *Subcommittee Staff Director*
ED FEDDEMAN *Professional Staff Member*
RUBEN VAN MITCHELL *Professional Staff Member*
KEN MONROE, *Professional Staff Member*
CHRIS SHANK *Professional Staff Member*
RICHARD OBERMANN *Democratic Professional Staff Member*
TOM HAMMOND *Staff Assistant*

U.S. SENATE
COMMITTEE ON COMMERCE, SCIENCE, AND
TRANSPORTATION

HON. JOHN MCCAIN, Arizona, *Chairperson*

TED STEVENS, Alaska
CONRAD BURNS, Montana
TRENT LOTT, Mississippi
KAY BAILEY HUTCHISON, Texas
OLYMPIA J. SNOWE, Maine
SAM BROWNBACK, Kansas
GORDON SMITH, Oregon
PETER G. FITZGERALD, Illinois
JOHN ENSIGN, Nevada
GEORGE ALLEN, Virginia
JOHN O. SUNUNU, New Hampshire

ERNEST F. HOLLINGS, South Carolina
DANIEL K. INOUYE, Hawaii
JOHN D. ROCKEFELLER IV, West Virginia
JOHN F. KERRY, Massachusetts
JOHN B. BREAUX, Louisiana
BYRON L. DORGAN, North Dakota

RON WYDEN, Oregon
BARBARA BOXER, California
BILL NELSON, Florida
MARIA CANTWELL, Washington
FRANK LAUTENBERG, New Jersey

FLOYD DESCHAMPS, *Republican Senior Professional Staff*
KEN LA SALA, *Republican Professional Staff*
JEAN TOAL EISEN, *Democratic Senior Professional Staff*

CONTENTS

from the State of New Jersey

Witness

Debris Assessment and Need for Imagery
Re-evaluating NASA's Mission
Lessons From the *Challenger* Investigation

Appendix 1: Answers to Post-Hearing Questions

Responses by the National Aeronautics and Space Administration (NASA)

Appendix 2: Additional Material for the Record

National Aeronautics and Space Administration Charter of the Aerospace Safety Advisory Panel, signed and dated May 1, 2003

SPACE SHUTTLE COLUMBIA

FEBRUARY 12, 2003

Subcommittee on Space and Aeronautics,

House of Representatives,

Committee on Science,

Joint with U.S. Senate,

Committee on Commerce, Science,

and Transportation,

Washington, DC.

The Committees met, pursuant to notice, at 9:35 a.m. in Room SR–325, Russell Senate Office Building, Hon. John McCain, Chairman of the Senate Committee, presiding.

OPENING STATEMENT OF HON. JOHN McCAIN, U.S. SENATOR FROM ARIZONA

Chairman **MCCAIN.** Good morning. I welcome my colleagues from the House Science Committee and Administrator O'Keefe.

To keep this hearing to a reasonable length, I appreciate my colleagues' indulgence in limiting opening statements only to those of the chairmen and Ranking Members of the Senate Committee on Commerce, Science, and Transportation and the House Science Committee.

Following Administrator O'Keefe's statement, all Members will be recognized for four minutes to ask questions. We will alternate between Senators and House Members for questions, which is the normal procedure in joint hearings of this nature.

On February 1st, the Nation suffered a devastating loss. As the Space Shuttle *Columbia* descended from orbit, it broke apart. Debris from the accident is still being collected by government agencies and volunteers with the hope that this evidence will help determine the cause of the accident.

The Space Shuttle crew was a remarkable team of professionals. They were and will always be role models for all Americans. Their dedicated service and sacrifice to promote scientific research not only for our country, but for the world, will never be forgotten. They paid the ultimate price in pursuit of not only their dreams, but the dreams of nations. For that, we will be forever grateful.

As we look to the future of the space program, we can pay tribute to our fallen heroes by diligently carrying out our responsibilities as legislators. In today's hearing, we hope to examine what went wrong on February 1st, the status of the investigation, and how we can ensure that an accident like this will never happen again.

This will be the first of a series of hearings on NASA and our space program. While today we're focusing on the *Columbia*, the accident also has focused our attention on the broader policy issues that perhaps we have neglected for too long. In subsequent hearings we will address the role of manned and unmanned space exploration, the costs and benefits of continuing the shuttle program, and our investment in the International Space Station and the effectiveness of NASA management. More fundamentally, we must examine the goals of our space program.

I firmly believe that manned space exploration should continue. Its nature, however, should be and will be examined. We also must examine the extent to which Congress and the Administration may have neglected the Shuttle's safety program. A comprehensive examination necessitates a review of our own actions and those of the Administration to determine if the Shuttle program was underfunded or managed in a manner that compromised safety.

I applaud Administrator Sean O'Keefe and NASA for their openness and availability. This has been an extraordinarily trying time for everyone in the agency. The Administrator and other officials have conducted themselves in a manner worthy of an agency that is not only a national brain trust, but is entrusted with realizing the dreams of all humanity. Many have noted the vast improvement of the release of information, as compared to the *Challenger* tragedy of 1986.

I would like to assure the families of the brave men and women who died aboard the *Columbia* and the dedicated employees of NASA that we will do everything in our power to identify the cause of this tragedy and remedy it.

I thank Administrator O'Keefe and his team for appearing before us today, and I look forward to the testimony.

STATEMENT OF HON. SHERWOOD L. BOEHLERT, U.S. REPRESENTATIVE FROM NEW YORK

Chairman **BOEHLERT.** We usually open hearings by talking about what a pleasure it is to be here today. But, of course, that is not the case. I'm reminded of what Lyndon Johnson said when he appeared before Congress after the Kennedy assassination. He said, "All I have, I gladly would have given not to be standing before you today." I'm sure that is the way we all feel with the tragic loss of the *Columbia* crew so fresh in our minds and in our hearts.

But we owe it to those astronauts and their families and to the American public to work as hard as humanly possible to determine the cause of the Shuttle's breakup and to rigorously pursue all the policy questions the accident brings to a head.

I view this hearing as a start of a very long conversation we will all be having about the *Columbia* incident and its ramifications. I think that it's very appropriate that we start that conversation on a bicameral basis, and I want to thank Senator McCain for being so willing to make this a Joint Hearing. The House and the Senate and NASA are going to have to cooperate as we each review the accident and the human space flight program, and our joint work today should send a clear signal that we can and will do just that.

We will also be coordinating with the *Columbia* Accident Investigation Board headed by Admiral Gehman. I've spoken to Admiral Gehman, and I am impressed with the Admiral's determination to be independent and deliberate, vowing to be swayed neither by outside pressures or artificial deadlines. And I appreciate the swiftness with which Administrator O'Keefe activated the board.

That said, the more I've read the board's charter, the more I've become convinced that it must be rewritten. The words of the charter simply do not guarantee the independence and latitude that both the Administrator and the Admiral have sincerely promised. The charter's words need to match everyone's intent now to avoid any problems later. I also continue to believe that several more members should be added to the board to ensure that it has the appropriate breadth of experience and expertise.

We will be working closely with the board as the Science Committee proceeds with its own bipartisan investigation, which will focus on the many policy questions raised by the accident. We're going to have to raise some tough and basic questions that have gone unanswered for too long.

What are the true risks of flying the Shuttle, especially if it's going to remain in service for another 10 to 15 years? What are the true costs of continuing the Shuttle program at specific levels of risk? And what are the advantages of investing in the Shuttle, as compared to investing in other NASA programs, other R&D programs, and, indeed, other government programs, in general?

But we can't begin to deal with those overarching issues until we have a better sense of what happened to the *Columbia* and why, and it's obviously too soon to expect to know that.

No one should expect any revelations at today's hearing. We are here today to get a status report. We ought to avoid pronouncements today that we may later come to regret.

I'm reminded of an interview I once read with an executive of the utility that owned Three Mile Island at the time of the accident there. He was asked, "What was the worst thing you did in handling the accident?" He answered immediately. He said, "We just didn't have the presence of mind to say, 'I don't know.' "

I would advise Administrator O'Keefe, who has responded magnificently in this time of crisis, don't hesitate to say, "I don't know." You're still in search of elusive answers.

Despite the best of intentions, NASA has at times already put out misleading information because it didn't check the facts. For example, information indicating that environmental rules could have contributed to the accident have so far turned out to be entirely spurious, but it's taken NASA a long time to clarify its statements.

Today is a chance to put facts into the record, facts that will help chart NASA's future. If we are to find the facts and honor the memory of the *Columbia* crew, we have to approach our task in a true spirit of exploration, with open and probing minds, without preconceived notions or foregone conclusions. That should be our goal today.

Thank you, Mr. Chairman.

[The prepared statement of Chairman Boehlert follows:]

PREPARED STATEMENT OF CHAIRMAN SHERWOOD L. BOEHLERT

We usually open hearings by talking about what a pleasure it is to be here. But of course today that is not the case. I'm reminded of what Lyndon Johnson said when he appeared before Congress after the Kennedy assassination: "All I have, I gladly would have given, not to be standing before you today." I'm sure that is the way we all feel, with the tragic loss of the *Columbia* crew so fresh in our minds and in our hearts.

But we owe it to those astronauts and their families, and to the American public, to work as hard as is humanly possible to determine the cause of the Shuttle's breakup and to rigorously pursue all the policy questions the accident brings to a head.

I view this hearing as the start of a very long conversation we will all be having about the *Columbia* incident and its ramifications. I think that it's very appropriate that we start that conversation on a bicameral basis, and I want to thank Senator McCain for being so open to making this a joint hearing. The House and the Senate and NASA are going to have to cooperate as we each review the accident and the Human Space Flight program, and our joint work today should send a clear signal that we can and will do just that.

We will also all be coordinating with the *Columbia* Accident Investigation Board, headed by Admiral Gehman. I spoke to Admiral Gehman earlier this week, as did our Committee staff on a bipartisan basis. I am impressed with the Admiral's determination to be independent and deliberate, vowing to be swayed neither by outside pressures or artificial deadlines. That's the right attitude, and we will be watching to ensure that it guides the Board's proceedings.

We will be working with Admiral Gehman as the Science Committee proceeds with its own bipartisan investigation, which will focus on the many policy questions raised by the accident. In the end, we must have a full appraisal and open debate about the true risks of flying the Shuttle, the true costs of continuing the Shuttle program at specific levels of risk, and the comparative advantages of investing in the Shuttle as opposed to other NASA programs, or indeed as opposed to other R&D programs or government programs, in general.

But we can't begin to deal with those overarching issues until we have a better sense of what happened to the *Columbia* and why, and it's obviously too soon to expect to know that. No one should expect any revelations at today's hearing. We are here today to get a status report.

We all ought to avoid pronouncements today that we may later come to regret. I'm reminded of an interview I once read with an executive of the utility that owned Three Mile Island at the time of the accident there. He was asked, "What was the worst thing you did in handling the accident?" He answered immediately. He said, "We just didn't have the presence of mind to say, 'I don't know.'" I would advise Administrator O'Keefe, who has responded magnificently in this time of crisis: don't hesitate to say, "I don't know."

Despite the best of intentions, NASA has already sometimes put out misleading information because it didn't check the facts. For example, information indicating that environmental rules could have contributed to the accident has so far turned out to be entirely spurious. But it's taken NASA a long time to clarify its statements.

One reason I believe that today's hearing can be useful is that with so much information is already floating around from so many sources, it's important that Congress and NASA have an opportunity to create a clear record of where things stand at this point.

It's especially important today that we get a clear sense of how NASA will handle the investigation and what contingency plans are in place should the Shuttle be grounded for an extended period of time. I'm sure we will also examine how NASA had been viewing the long-range safety of the Shuttle prior to the accident and how this may already have changed.

All of us are still mourning the loss of the *Columbia* crew, but we must now turn to planning the future. And we can do that only in a true spirit of exploration—with a full and open examination of all the facts, without preconceived notions or foregone conclusions. That process starts today. Thank you.

Chairman **MCCAIN.** Senator Hollings.

STATEMENT OF HON. ERNEST O. HOLLINGS, U.S. SENATOR FROM SOUTH CAROLINA

Senator **HOLLINGS.** Thank you very much, Mr. Chairman, for calling this meeting. We welcome our colleagues from the House side and my old friend, Administrator O'Keefe. We're glad to have you with us.

Chairman Boehlert, I got the message, "Let's don't jump to conclusions." I'm reading in the morning paper a similar message—Admiral Gehman said that "the investigation with solid evidence thus far hard to come by." On the contrary, we have a lot of solid evidence that we've come by, and I sort of discern some kind of eery avoidance here of what really happened.

Here is the hard evidence. NASA's had a long history of problems with the Shuttle's heat tiles. We know that the *Columbia*'s VERY first mission, many of the tiles flew off. That's 22 years ago. In 1994, a study entitled the *Risk Management for the Tiles of the Space Shuttle,* by Stanford and Carnegie Mellon University, found that 15 percent of the Shuttle's tiles account for 85 percent of the risk. And that was confirmed by a 1997 study by the National Academy of Sciences.

Then a study by the Johnson Space Center in March of 2000 found that the leading edges of the wing, quote, "pose the highest risk for critical failure," end quote. And then during the launch of the *Columbia* on January the 16th, we have video evidence of debris striking the Shuttle orbiter 81 seconds after launch, potentially causing a gash in the left wing of some 30 inches long, seven inches wide, and over two-and-a-half inches thick. And then 18 minutes from landing, the Shuttle was pitching and yawing due to drag on the left wing.

And, of course, this morning's paper says that as it was coming down, and I'm quoting the Mission Control, "FYI," for your information, "I've just lost four separate temperature transducers on the left side of the vehicle, hydraulic return temperatures," he calmly reported.

Again quoting, eight minutes before all communications was lost, Mr. Kling noticed the loss of data from temperature gauges on the left wing on the spacecraft as he monitored the Shuttle's descent into the atmosphere. A few moments later, Mr. Kling reported drag on the spaceship, but controllers expressed no alarm.

And, finally, the elevons, the picture that showed the elevons, tried to counteract that drag in engine thrusters to help it gain control, because a minute before the explosion, the U.S. Air Force captured that picture of the Shuttle showing a bulge of deformity along the front edge of the left wing. Right on down the list.

Mr. Administrator, I would think, in the testimony, we all agree that we don't want to jump to conclusions. We all agree to be very thorough and leave no stone unturned, but we do have a rebuttable presumption here that the damage to the left wing at the time of liftoff was the cause. And let's rebut it. Let's find something. But don't all of a sudden be discovering debris all around and all of these other things that pant one way and say we have no idea what happened.

I have been in these investigations before, and we knew exactly what happened at the *Challenger*. Allen McDonald said he was in the control room. They had warned not to take it off. It was going to cause a catastrophe. And he said one gentlemen said, "There she goes." Another one said, "Like a piece of cake." Then he said it exploded, and everyone in the room knew why. We spent years investigating to find out the same thing that we knew immediately at the time of explosion.

Thank you, Mr. Chairman.

[The prepared statement of Senator Hollings follows:]

PREPARED STATEMENT OF SENATOR ERNEST O. HOLLINGS

I would like to begin by offering my condolences to the family members of the Space Shuttle *Columbia* crew of mission STS–107. These heroes gave their lives in the advancement of science and all Americans should be overwhelmed by their sacrifice. The *Columbia* crew was on a special mission to conduct scientific research in outer space. As a strong supporter of scientific research, I'm grateful to all the men and women of NASA who undertake such endeavors to advance scientific knowledge.

Welcome Administrator O'Keefe. You are here today to provide my distinguished colleagues and I with answers of how this tragedy was allowed to happen. There is a question as to whether this committee has consistently provided NASA with the funds it has requested for the Space Shuttle program. We want to get to the bottom of this accident so that we can ensure that it does not happen again.

Now I know that the NASA engineers have developed this "fault tree" to identify all the possible causes of this tragic event. Branches are continually added, but nothing is eliminated. Investigators are exploring every lead, but the facts of the matter are:

We have video evidence of debris striking the Shuttle orbiter 81 seconds after launch. Engineers estimated the damaged tile area in the *left wing* to be 30 inches long by 7 inches wide, yet there was no concern for the tiles failing upon re-entry into the Earth's atmosphere.

NASA's had a long history of problems with the heat tiles. These problems date back to 1981 when the first *Columbia* launch came back with lost or damaged tiles.

NASA has recognized the tile problem. Numerous studies have been conducted. In 1990 a study found that *15 percent of the Shuttle's tiles account for 85 percent of its risks* and recommended that improving maintenance procedures could reduce the probability of tile related Shuttle accidents by 70 percent.

Less than 18 minutes from landing, the Shuttle was pitching and yawing due to drag on the *left wing.* Its elevons tried to counteract the drag and engine thrusters had fired to gain control.

It is clear that we have a rebuttable presumption to go forward with the investigation to focus the examination on how the tiles failed causing the catastrophic failure.

Chairman **MCCAIN.** Thank you, Senator Hollings.

Congressman Hall hasn't arrived yet, so we will proceed to Mr. O'Keefe, the Administrator of the National Aeronautics and Space Administration. He's accompanied by Mr. Frederick D. Gregory, who is the Deputy Administrator, and Mr. William Reedy, the Associate Administrator for Space Flight. If you'd like to join—or they can remain where they are.

And, again, I want to thank you for the extreme willingness on your part to share all information that you have with not only Members of Congress, but with the American people.

Please proceed, Mr. O'Keefe, and I hope you understand that we're interested in as thorough a briefing as possible, as are Americans who are viewing this hearing today.

Thank you.

[The prepared statement of Senator Lautenberg follows:]

PREPARED STATEMENT OF SENATOR FRANK R. LAUTENBERG

Mr. Chairman,

Today's hearing on the Space Shuttle *Columbia* disaster and the hearings likely to follow in the weeks and months ahead will bring additional pain to that which we already feel while in a period of mourning for seven brave, exceptional human beings in the prime of life. The hearings will also bring pain because, frankly, indications are that some earlier warnings might have raised questions about whether or not presumption of risk was insufficiently reviewed.

The Space Shuttle *Columbia* disaster forces us to ask difficult questions. The Federal Government has spent more than $60 billion on the Space Shuttle program, the International Space Station, and the X–33/VentureStar Space Plane (which advocates believed would replace the Shuttle). Our fleet of Shuttles is grounded at least until we determine what caused the *Columbia* accident and fix it; the three-person crew of the Space Station spends 80 percent of their time on maintenance; and the Bush Administration has canceled the Space Plane project. As a result of that cancellation, we now intend to continue using Shuttles at least until 2012, and possibly beyond 2020. Some of the technology on the Shuttles is 30 years old. We never intended to use them this long.

I want to make it clear that I feel that the Shuttle astronauts made a major contribution to our effort to assess the value to humankind of research in space, and I grieve over their deaths. The desire to reach for the stars is as old as human history and the ambitions embodied in our manned space program are noble ones. But we have had two fatal accidents in 113 Shuttle missions. Many people have become inured to the dangers inherent in sending people into space and bringing them back safely. But the fact is, it's a high-risk venture. Some risk is unavoidable—that's what makes our astronauts such brave individuals. But are we willing to divert precious resources available for other essential research and experimentation planned or in place to reduce the risks of manned space exploration to the point where they become acceptable?

Because of the downturn in the economy that started in March 2001, the September 11th terrorist attacks, and the tax cuts enacted that year, we are facing federal budget deficits "as far as the eye can see." And now the Administration proposes to reduce federal revenues even more. How can we guarantee that we can spend what it takes to make the space effort safer and successful? If we make the investment necessary, what benefits will we reap from continued Shuttle operations? What are the "opportunity costs" of such an investment? In other words, what other national priorities will suffer in the battle for scarce funds? Our manned space exploration program has been long on ambition but increasingly short on the hard-headed assessments needed to answer these fundamental questions.

Manned space exploration isn't cheap. If we try to do it on the cheap, we put safety—and people's lives—at risk. I'm sure we will hear in testimony today and in the future that safety has never been compromised. But NASA has always had problems overseeing its contractors. And the National Research Council has concluded that the contract to manage the Shuttle program awarded to United Space Alliance in 1996 contained financial incentives for investments in efficiency, but not for investments in modernization and safety improvements.

Much of today's hearing and the hearings to come will focus on technical matters—possible causes of the *Columbia* accident, possible safety improvements. I am interested to know, for instance, what steps—if any—NASA took to ensure *Columbia's* safe re-entry after determining that debris—presumably foam insulation from the fuel tank—hit and may have damaged the left win during lift-off. I am also interested in learning from NASA Administrator Sean O'Keefe what additional safety precautions might have been assured with greater funding. And I want to know what safety upgrades, if any, were made after the *Columbia* space flights scheduled for August 2000 and March 2002 were postponed.

In the course of today's hearing and future hearings, we will also scrutinize NASA's relationship with its contractors. We will also review Congress's relationship with NASA. We will analyze Administration budget requests for NASA past and present.

I hope our investigation will be more about fixing problems than fixing blame—although determining accountability obviously is important. But beyond such immediate concerns, I hope we will address the harder question about whether the benefits outweigh the risks when we send people into space at this time and in the current fashion when unmanned missions can almost entirely match the quality of human participation.

[The prepared statement of Ms. Jackson Lee follows:]

PREPARED STATEMENT OF REPRESENTATIVE SHEILA JACKSON LEE

Mr. Chairman,

Thank you for calling this hearing and bringing us all together to speak and learn about the *Columbia* tragedy. This is a tough time for all of us from the Houston community, but especially for the team at Johnson Space Center. To the world those astronauts were valiant heroes; to us they were also friends, neighbors, and family—or as the Houston Chronicle proclaimed them, "The Heroes Next Door." I am impressed by the diligence, progress, and openness of the NASA investigators that we have all been getting to know through the press.

Those investigators have a difficult job ahead, and it is essential that that job be done well. We must find all the available facts, and we must not jump to hasty conclusions. It seems that the data is pouring in, in the form of video, computer analysis and collection of debris. I am concerned by reports of loose foam or ice that may have damaged the left wing during liftoff, especially since this may have been a problem in a past mission. I want to know what was done to keep such chunks from detaching and striking our multi-billion dollar Shuttle, entrusted with the lives of 7 Americans.

However, we cannot be myopic and disregard or short-change other evidence and explanations. The inquiries must be methodical and objective. The team must leave no room for suspicion of cover-up or sloppiness. The families of the seven valiant crew members that lost loved ones deserve to know why this tragedy happened, as do the American people. Most importantly, we owe it to our brave future astronauts to show them our commitment to their safety.

I am pleased that after we Democrats in the Science Committee sent a letter to the President expressing our concerns about the independence of the investigatory board, that the hearing and make-up of the board were changed. However, I feel there is still room for improvement. I recommend the inclusion of Nobel Laureates, academicians, and depending on their interests—perhaps family members of lost crew. It is important that the team is weighted toward bright people, who are not employees of NASA, and who do not have close personal ties to NASA or the Administrator.

The conclusions we all reach must not only be in the form of, "Part A broke, and part B got too hot." We must discern what were the factors that led to those parts being included in a vehicle entrusted with seven lives and such an important mission. What were the quality assurance protocols? Were corners cut?

Furthermore, this investigation needs to be expeditious. We have three Space Shuttles with critical missions already planned. We also have the International Space Station, with three astronauts high up above us waiting to hear their own futures. Thankfully, we have partnered with our Russian allies and others and ensured that we have the means to get those astronauts home, even though we may need to ground our own fleet for some time. However, we cannot continually place American lives in the hands of another nation for long. Nor can we risk losing the use of the International Space Station that we have been working so hard, and investing so much, to achieve.

[The prepared statement of Ms. Lofgren follows:]

PREPARED STATEMENT OF REPRESENTATIVE ZOE LOFGREN

I'd like to thank Congressman Boehlert and Senator McCain for convening this hearing. Over the next few months, we will be asking some tough questions related to the breakup and loss of the *Columbia,* and the future of the United States space program. But first, our country has paused to reflect on the heroism of the seven astronauts who gave their lives so that the dreams of humans reaching for the stars can live forever. My thoughts go out to the families of our fallen, and to the extended NASA family.

I am pleased the NASA Administrator Sean O'Keefe has joined us here today. I look forward to hearing from and working with you and the dedicated and hard working members of the NASA employee family, as we seek answers to our concerns about the future of the United States space program. I trust that you will ask us for help, keep us informed and be prepared to make your recommendations to this committee that will help us be able to move our space program forward. I firmly believe this committee must focus on asking the difficult questions that relate to how we are best able to resume our quest to explore space.

This committee must work in a nonpartisan manner and should not waste any time in trying to assess blame or create excuses for things that should have been done to help prevent this immense tragedy and loss. To do so would be a waste of time and money and, more importantly, would dishonor the sacrifices made of the brave *Columbia* crew and devalue the efforts being made by all who seek to ensure that this never happens again.

I believe that our pursuit of answers to this tragedy would best be served by the appointment of a truly independent board of inquiry, much like President Reagan appointed after the *Challenger* disaster. Until that happens, Mr. O'Keefe, I am pleased that you accepted some of the recommendations contained in a letter sent to the President last week by 16 Democratic members of the House Science Committee. I am sure many of our Republican colleagues would have joined us in expressing our concerns about the composition of the review board, and I am confident they would have echoed our concerns. Without these changes, I believe the results of this work would have been viewed with great skepticism and certainly would have suffered without the added, independent expertise of the new members of the board. Just as *Columbia*'s crew went into space seeking to expand our knowledge of space, we must do all in our power to ensure that our investigations will answer more questions than they create.

Mr. Chairman, I am committed to sending humans into space. We are explorers by nature, and I believe we must explore our own planet and those beyond. I believe these hearings need to focus not only on investigating the policy concerns that led to the Shuttle tragedy, but where we go from here in the exploration of space.

Has NASA shifted monies to the ISS and away from the Shuttle program?

Are we going to develop the next generation of space vehicle, and should we pursue a single-stage-to-orbit program?

Should we also develop the use of expendable rockets to ferry equipment and personnel to the International Space Station?

Are we prepared to fund this program—as I think we should—in the current budget climate?

With this in mind, I believe this committee can best honor the memory of *Columbia*'s crew by conducting an honest examination of the role, if any, of recent budget cuts played in this disaster. Should we take this opportunity to acknowledge that the Space Shuttle has never lived up to its dreams of being a cost effective way of traveling to space? Or are we better served by pursuing a new generation of space vehicles, one that can take advantage of the tremendous advances in our knowledge and our technologies than those present in the remaining Shuttle fleet?

STATEMENT OF SEAN O'KEEFE, ADMINISTRATOR, NATIONAL AERONAUTICS AND SPACE ADMINISTRATION; ACCOMPANIED BY FREDERICK D. GREGORY, DEPUTY ADMINISTRATOR, AND WILLIAM O. READDY, ASSOCIATE ADMINISTRATOR FOR SPACE FLIGHT

Mr. **O'KEEFE.** Good morning. Thank you, Mr. Chairman, Chairman Boehlert.

I appreciate the opportunity to appear before this hearing of the Senate Commerce, Science, and Transportation Committee and the House Science Subcommittee on Space and Aeronautics to discuss the tragic loss of the courageous crew of the Space Shuttle

Columbia——

Chairman **MCCAIN.** Could you pull the microphone a little closer?

Mr. **O'KEEFE.** —the ongoing investigation into this tragedy and the implications of the loss of *Columbia* to the Nation's space exploration efforts.

This morning, 11 days after the accident, our work continues to honor the solemn pledge we made to the astronauts' families and to the American people, that we'll find out what caused the loss of the *Columbia* and its crew, correct what problems we find, and do our utmost to make sure this never happens again.

We welcome the Joint Committee's interest in working with NASA to determine how we can learn from this tragic accident so that we continue advancing the Nation's research and exploration objectives in space while at the same time striving to ensure that we make human space flight as safe as possible.

Throughout NASA's 45 years of serving the public interest, Congress has been our partner helping us achieve the goals outlined in NASA's congressionally authorized charter. This charter compels NASA to explore, use, and enable the development of space for human enterprise; advance scientific knowledge and understanding of the Earth, the solar system, and the universe; and use the environment of space for research; research, develop, verify, and transfer advanced aeronautics, space, and related technologies.

With the support of Congress, NASA has amassed a record of significant achievements that have tangibly improved the lives of all Americans. And when we have erred, you have helped us right our course.

This morning, you'll be asking tough questions, and that's as it should be. Believe me, none of the questions that you will ask can be any tougher than those we're asking of ourselves. I can assure you, however, that whatever determinations are reached regarding the cause of the accident, you'll find that complacency is not one of them.

An ethos of safety is evident throughout the agency. For example, last year we temporarily halted Shuttle flight operations when tiny cracks of less than two inches were discovered in metal liners used to direct the fuel flow inside the propellent lines on two separate orbiters. We did not fly again until that problem was corrected. In a signal of our continuing commitment to rewarding such diligence, we also made it a point to praise a very young examiner, a fellow named David Strait, the young contract employee who had actually discovered the cracks.

Other flight decisions made throughout the year were made with the goal of operational safety being paramount. And from working with the dedicated employees who keep the Shuttle flying safely, I know they have the utmost regard for the enormity of that duty.

This week, at NASA centers throughout the country and in the field, with the support of more than 2,000 people from more than 20 federal agencies, state and local organizations, the important work of data analysis and recovery operations is continuing. We should all be extremely proud of the work that's being conducted by these dedicated public servants.

President Bush observed last week, "The people of NASA are being tested once again. In your grief, you are responding as your friends would have wished, with focus, professionalism, and unbroken faith in the mission of this agency. Captain Brown was correct, America's space program will go on." We intend to maintain that professionalism he referred to until we reach conclusion and beyond.

This morning, to help frame our discussion, I'd like to review for you the significant actions NASA has taken since the morning of the accident in accord with our contingency plan. In addition to articulating notification of first-response procedures defining the roles and responsibility of mishap response and Mishap Investigation Teams, the plan specifies selections of persons outside of NASA to head an independent, seasoned, accident investigation team. Now, while we did not foresee this tragedy, our response has unfolded as we had planned and prepared for in that contingency plan that we had hoped to never have to activate.

This plan was one of many positive outcomes from the terrible loss of the Space Shuttle *Challenger* 17 years ago. So we developed the plan shortly after that and have updated it before every flight. And a contingency was simulated for this very event just three months ago.

When we first became aware of the problems with STS–107, I was waiting at the Space Shuttle landing strip at the Kennedy Space Center, Cape Canaveral, on Saturday morning, February the 1st. At 8:59 a.m. eastern time, we lost communication with the *Columbia*. At 9:16, the countdown arrival clock reached zero, and there was no signal or sign of the *Columbia*. Captain Bill Readdy, our Associate Administrator for Space Flight and a former astronaut, declared a space flight contingency and activated the recovery control center at the Kennedy Space Center. At that point, Bill Readdy and I departed the landing strip and headed to the launch control center.

We arrived at the launch control center 13 minutes later. At 9:29 a.m., we activated the contingency action plan for space flight operations. Through the White House situation room, we notified the President as well as other senior staff of the loss of communications. In addition, Members of Congress and the Government of Israel were notified. Homeland Security Secretary

Tom Ridge and the National Security Council were also made aware of the situation and were present there in the situation room that morning.

Secretary Ridge then began assessing the possibility that this situation was terrorism related. Shortly after, he made the determination it was highly unlikely terrorism was involved. Secretary Ridge then announced that the Federal Emergency Management Agency would be the lead federal agency for the recovery effort on the ground.

Meanwhile, the family members of the *Columbia* astronauts were escorted from the landing strip to the astronauts' crew quarters. Later that morning, at about 11:30, we met with the families at the crew quarters at Kennedy Space Center to express our condolences, offer any and all support we could give, and assure them that we would offer that support throughout this entire ordeal, and stated our commitment to find the cause of the accident, fix the problems we find, and continue the work that their loved ones had started.

Data at all the NASA sites and contractors were impounded at 10 a.m., and the headquarters action team in Washington, D.C., was activated with NASA personnel moving immediately to their duty stations. By 10:30, an hour after the contingency plan had been activated, the mishap response team convened to assess the preliminary data and focus on the location of the crew compartment through the Rescue Coordination Center at Langley Air Force Base in Virginia. The rapid response team was activated for deployment to Barksdale Air Force Base in Louisiana that day.

The process of initiating the *Columbia* Accident Investigation Board began about 10:30 a.m. on Saturday, February 1st, one hour after the contingency plan was activated. I placed a call to the NASA deputy administrator, Fred Gregory, also a former astronaut, who was at NASA headquarters in Washington. Mr.

Gregory then began calling the *Columbia* Accident Investigation Board members, which are specified by position in the contingency action plan.

At 1:15 that afternoon, I made a brief televised statement expressing our national regrets for the tragic accident and informed the public about the appointment of the *Columbia* Accident Investigation Board.

The Accident Investigation Board was formally activated during the NASA Mishap Investigation Team teleconference, which occurred at 5 p.m. that afternoon, Saturday, February the 1st, less than eight hours after the event.

By 6 p.m., during a teleconference with the White House situation room, we briefed officials from the Department of Homeland Security, the Federal Emergency Management Agency, the Department of Defense, the FBI, and the Federal Aviation Administration about the current status of the accident investigation.

At 6:40 that evening, staff members of the National Transportation Safety Board departed Washington and traveled to Barksdale Air Force Base in Louisiana to assist as part of the Mishap Investigation Team, that day. They were later made available to the *Columbia* Accident Investigation Board.

On Sunday, February the 2nd, the Accident Investigation Board, chaired by retired United States Navy Admiral Hal Gehman, held its first meeting at Barksdale Air Force Base in Louisiana, less than 30 hours after the accident. We also began the practice of twice-daily briefings at headquarters in Washington and at the Johnson Space Center in Houston.

Membership of the *Columbia* Accident Investigation Board consists of persons selected for their positions in heading civil and military offices with responsibility for aerospace safety, accident investigations, and related skills. Many have been chief investigators on major accidents. And between them, board members have the experience of some 50 major investigations to draw upon. Quite simply, the people who are now on the board are some of the best in the world at what they do, and they were activated immediately. You have our assurance that this distinguished board will be able to act with genuine independence.

When the board assembled, it modified its charter to eliminate any reference to NASA directing the administration of the investigation. The framework that was contained in the contingency plan was modified and will continue to be to ensure the independence of this board. NASA accepted the changes to the charter without objection, as I will continue to do in the future, as well, for any changes they propose.

Further, the NASA Inspector General Robert Cobb is an observer on the *Columbia* Accident Investigation Board, having arrived on Monday, February the 3rd. He will help assure the independence of the board, as he reports both to the President and to the Congress under the terms of the Inspector General Act.

There are additional details about the *Columbia* Accident Investigation Board and its activities that are, I think, important to note. The board has taken over hardware and software releases of NASA so that we cannot alter anything unless the board approves. We've already begun to honor document requests from the board, as we have all along, and have also supplied additional documents to the board which were not requested, but we believe might be helpful in their work as we move along. And, finally, the board has instructed NASA to conduct a fault-tree analysis that it intends to independently validate, to look at all the possible causes that could have occurred and to examine those in a very methodical way, which they will then, in turn, independently validate.

On Sunday, the NASA Mishap Investigation Team was on the ground and working with local officials in Texas and Louisiana. The State of Texas activated 800 members of the Texas National Guard to assist with the retrieval of debris, and I am eternally grateful to Governor Rick Perry for his immediate response within hours of our request.

By Tuesday, there were nearly 200 NASA and NASA contractor personnel working recovery operations in Texas, Louisiana, Arizona, and California. They were part of the more than 2,000 people from Federal Emergency Management Agency, the Environmental Protection Agency, the FBI, the Department of Defense, Department of Transportation, the U.S. Forest Service, Texas National Guard, Louisiana National Guard, and state and local authorities working to locate, document, and collect debris.

By Wednesday, the astronauts' remains were transferred to Dover Air Force Base in Delaware. At Dover, NASA Deputy Administrator Fred Gregory, and former astronaut, and ceremonial honor guard were present to pay our respect to the seven fallen astronauts.

Throughout the week, we were able to make steady progress in our efforts to recover debris from the accident. We have, thus far, recovered upwards of 12,000 elements of debris. The search effort, as you know from our press conferences, is a large, complex, and ongoing effort with hundreds of square miles with challenging weather and terrain conditions. And, indeed, the graphic that's up now is that 500-mile swath from Dallas/Fort Worth area to just south of Shreveport, Louisiana, in and around the Lufkin, Texas, area.

We're very grateful that no one was injured on the ground as a result of flying debris from the accident, and we're working with our agency partners to assure recovery operations remain safe as we continue this effort.

Throughout the course of this activity, I've also briefed the President and the Vice President on a near-daily basis to advise and apprise them of all the progress we're making, as well as the cooperation of all of the federal agencies, who have been extremely participating in this effort.

The Federal Emergency Management Agency command post was set up in Lufkin, Texas, on Saturday, the 1st of February, and has been operating nonstop since then. Debris collection activities began at Barksdale Air Force Base on Sunday, February the 2nd.

Yesterday, we began transporting debris on trucks to the Kennedy Space Center where they'll be assembled and analyzed as part of the comprehensive accident investigation directed by the Gehman board.

I visited Texas and Louisiana this past Saturday to get my own assessment of the operation, but, more importantly, to personally thank the volunteers, in addition to all the federal, state, and local public servants, who have been working so tirelessly to support the debris recovery effort.

Let me touch briefly on the Space Shuttle fleet as it is today. *Discovery* is continuing to undergo major inspections and upgrades, which will be completed by April of 2004. *Atlantis* is currently assembled and stacked in a Vehicle Assembly Building at the Kennedy Space Center for STS–114, the next mission due to have, or planned to have, been flown. The *Endeavour,* the third of the orbiters, is in the Orbiter Processing Facility and being prepared for STS–115, which was scheduled a couple of months later.

The next Shuttle mission, STS–114, was to have been to the International Space Station in March, that mission commanded by

Colonel Eileen Collins, United States Air Force. And I met with her on Friday to further advise that the mission is on hold until we understand the causes of the *Columbia* accident and are able to resolve any issues identified.

At this time, we don't know how long it will be before we can resume Shuttle flights. We will only know when the *Columbia* Accident Investigation Board concludes its work and presents its findings to all of us.

Columbia was the first orbiter in the Shuttle fleet, having flown 28 successful missions, or just over a quarter of its certified life of a hundred flights. In February 2001, a little over a year ago, *Columbia* completed a major scheduled 18-month overhaul and update of its systems, a process we call "Orbiter Major Modifications." The STS–107 mission was *Columbia*'s second flight following that major overhaul. A successful servicing mission that had been conducted, the first one, was to the Hubble Space Telescope in March of 2002. So this was the second flight after it had been nearly completely rebuilt.

Prior to the loss of *Columbia* and her crew, the projected Shuttle flight rate was five per year, starting in 2004, and funding is requested for that flight rate in the budget the President just submitted last week. The flight rate will be adjusted as needed, of course, once we determine when we can return to flight safely.

The crew of the International Space Station is, of course, deeply saddened by the loss of *Columbia* and her crew, as are all of our partners and people around the world. I spoke with International Space Station crew members, Ken Bowersox, the commander, United States Navy, Don Pettit, who is our science officer aboard, and Nikolai Budarin, who is a cosmonaut engineer, on Sunday, February the 2nd for the first time in our discussions, to inform them of the accident and how we're proceeding. Despite the tragedy, the crew is continuing its busy schedule of work.

The day after the loss of STS–107, our Russian partners conducted a successful planned launch of an unmanned, autonomous Progress resupply vehicle to the station. The provisions carried on Progress 10P should provide the crew sufficient supplies to maintain normal operations through June 2003, through this summer. Progress resupply flights to the International Space Station by our Russian partners will continue as scheduled. The next flight is scheduled for June 2003.

We're working with Rosaviakosmos, the Russian Aviation and Space Agency officials, to determine what we might want to place on that flight to make sure we have the best use of the space available. In addition, a regularly scheduled Soyuz crew transport vehicle exchange is planned already for the launch in April 2003, as it had been prior to February 1st.

Study teams formed almost immediately after the accident to assess the impact on the International Space Station. These teams are focused on how we will, first, sustain the station, second, continue to assemble the station, as it is not yet complete, and, third, to maximize the utilization of this unique research platform.

We have kept our International Space Station partners informed of our recovery efforts. Further, we have met with our international partners just last week, and continue to each day, to plan future meetings in the weeks ahead to develop an International Space Station partner plan.

We can maintain a permanent crew on the International Space Station as long as it is necessary, with support from Soyuz and Progress flights. The International Space Station is stable and has sufficient propellent to maintain its orbit for at least a year without support from the Space Shuttle.

But the nearer-term issue for crew support beyond June is water. The International Space Station cannot support a crew of three after June with the currently planned support in progress. As a consequence, we're discussing with our international partners the possibility of changing the April Soyuz flight from a taxi mission to a crew exchange mission, as well as the feasibility of adding Progress resupply flights. But I want to really emphasize that there are no decisions that have been made, and all options are being examined at present.

I talked to the Expedition 6 crew that Captain Bowersix commands, now in orbit, and they've expressed determination and desire to do whatever is necessary to continue the research and deal with any changes in crew rotation schedule that may be necessary.

As we look forward to determine our nation's best course of action in responding to the *Columbia* accident, I'd like to point out that NASA developed an Integrated Space Transportation Plan, which was submitted by the President to the Congress in November as an amendment to the fiscal year 2003 budget. So three months ago, that plan was presented at that time. The Integrated Space Transportation Plan could help us address many of the near-term issues we're facing, even though it was developed prior to the loss of *Columbia*.

The plan reflects the tight coupling required across the Space Station, Space Shuttle, and the Space Launch Initiatives. It is intended to ensure that necessary access to the International Space Station can be supported for the foreseeable future. It consists of three major program elements—the Space Shuttle, the Orbital Space Plane, and the Next-Generation Launch Technology.

This new plan makes investments to extend Shuttle's operational life for continued safe operations. The Orbital Space Plane is designed to provide a crew transfer capability as early as possible to assure access to and from the International Space Station. And the Next-Generation Launch Technology program funds next-generation Reusable Launch Vehicle technology in areas such as propulsion, structures, and operation. This initiative will focus on the Orbital Space Plane and the Next-Generation Launch Technology, including third-generation Reusable Launch Vehicle efforts.

Now, the 2003 budget amendment that the President submitted last November, in 2002, also proposed adding funds to International Space Station reserves to assure that we could successfully reach the milestone of U.S. core configuration and maintain progress on the long lead items for enhanced research aboard space station and the continued buildout of that remarkable research laboratory platform.

Space flight is a means to an end at NASA. That end is research, exploration, discovery, and inspiration. The crew of STS–107 were engaged in a wide array of scientific research that could be conducted nowhere else but in space and had significant potential benefits for the public. *Columbia*'s crew took great pride in their research aimed at fighting cancer, improving crop yields, developing fire-suppression techniques, building earthquake-resistant buildings, and understanding the effects of dust storms on weather. As was recorded by the media, *Columbia* had a cargo of human ingenuity.

The crew of International Space Station is also conducting research now that cannot be conducted anywhere else. Thus far, more than 60 experiments spanning such scientific disciplines as human physiology, genetics, plant biology, Earth observations, physics, and cell biology have been conducted on the International Space Station. From these experiments, scientists are learning better methods of drug testing and about dynamic models of human diseases, the physics of fundamental processes in manufacturing, antibiotic synthesis, and changes in Earth climate, vegetation and crops.

The International Space Station is the centerpiece initiative of human space flight at NASA. Our objectives in this regard are very clear. First, we will keep on-orbit International Space Stations crews safe. Second, we intend to keep the International Space Station continuously occupied in order to assure the reliability of the station itself. And, third, we intend to return to assembly—as soon as we're able, to return the Shuttle fleet to safe operations and complete the research goals for ourselves and for our international partners.

To accomplish these aims, we need to create a long-term crew-return capability to complement and augment the Soyuz vehicles now provided by our partners. We intend to build that new return capability to create a new crew-transfer system that will allow us to rotate crews on the International Space Station independent from the Space Shuttle.

We also firmly believe that extending the operational life of the remaining Shuttle fleet is a good investment, because it will help maximize the science return from the International Space Station.

We designed our Integrated Space Transportation Plan to ensure that we have coordinated resources to exploit the unique research environment of space and the International Space Station in the near-, mid-, and long-term. We thought the plan was a good one when we proposed it, and we believe that it's not only valid today, but even more compelling to pursue. While we believe that this plan is a good one, we will re-examine it as necessary in light of the investigative findings of *Columbia*.

Just over a week ago, although it seemed more like a lifetime, the President spoke so eloquently and powerfully at the Johnson Space Center memorial service in Houston, Texas. He said, "The cause of exploration and discovery is not an option we choose; it is a desire written in the human heart. We're all part of a creation which seeks to understand all creation. **We find the best among us, send them forth into unmapped darkness, and pray they will return. They go in peace for all mankind, and all mankind is in their debt."**

The noble purposes described in the President's words frame all that we do and how we do it. These purposes drive our mission goals, which are to understand and protect our home planet, to explore the universe and search for life, and to inspire the next generation of explorers as only NASA can.

And even while our nonstop work to recover from this terrible tragedy and to continue safe operations on the International Space Station will be our chief focus in the days and weeks and months ahead, the American people should know we will also press ahead with other activities to achieve these important goals.

This centennial flight year, we are launching the Mars exploration rovers, the Mars spacecraft, the space infrared telescope facility, and a number of Earth science spacecraft and instruments, as well as continuing our work to help improve aviation security on behalf of our homeland defense. In these activities and in all that we do at NASA, we strive for unmatched excellence. When it comes to human space exploration, those margins are razor thin, and we know we're graded on an extremely harsh curve. For us, 96 percent to 99 percent is not an "A." One-hundred percent is the minimum passing garde.

Now, despite this harsh truth, we know the lesson from this terrible accident is not to turn our backs on exploration because it is hard or risky. **John Shedd once said about the age of ocean exploration, "A ship in safe harbor is safe, but that is not what**

ships are built for."

Human history teaches us that in exploration, after accidents like this occur, we learn from them and further reduce risks, although we must honestly admit that risk can never be eliminated.

President John F. Kennedy observed once, some 41 years ago, speaking of our fledgling space program at that time, "All great and honorable actions are accompanied with great difficulties, and both must be enterprised and overcome with answerable courage."

The immediate task before our agency is clear. We'll find the problem that caused the loss of *Columbia* and its crew, we'll fix it, and then we'll return to flight operations that are as safe as humanly possible in pursuit of knowledge. We have no preconceptions about what caused the failure or what it will take to make it so that it will never happen again. We have an independent Accident Investigation Board of truly outstanding and eminently quality individuals, and they, and only they alone, will determine the cause of the accident and its remedy, no matter where it leads. We're ready and willing to support the addition of any experts that Admiral Gehman deems necessary to the effective conduct of the board's investigations.

Part of my job as Administrator is to remind folks of what NASA does and what we are capable of doing. It's a responsibility I take very, very seriously. And, at the same time, I am saddened beyond words at the loss of seven outstanding men and women of STS–107. I'm also very proud and humbled by the focus, dedication, and professionalism of the NASA family and all those throughout the country who are assisting in this challenging recovery effort.

Today, February the 12th, is also the birthday of President Lincoln. And some of his words, spoken for an entirely different purpose, have come to mind this past week. "It is rather for us to be here dedicated to the great task remaining before us, that from these honored dead we take increase devotion to that cause for which they gave the last full measure of devotion."

We have an opportunity here and now to learn from this loss and renew the boundless spirit of exploration present at NASA's beginning. We will do this by being accountable to the American people for our failings and, we hope, credible and compelling in pursuit of research, exploration, and inspiration for future generations.

And, finally, during the 16-day STS–107 mission, we had no indication that would suggest a compromise to flight safety. The time it has taken me to present this testimony is about the same amount of time that transpired between when mission control first noticed anomalies in temperature measurements and the accident.

(Pause.)

I just paused for a few seconds. That's the same amount of time that transpired from mission control's last communication with the crew and our loss of signal with the heroic *Columbia* astronauts.

May Good bless the crew of STS–107.

Chairman McCain, Chairman Boehlert, thank you all very much for you attention.

[The prepared statement of Mr. O'Keefe follows:]

PREPARED STATEMENT OF SEAN O'KEEFE

Good morning. I appreciate the opportunity to appear before this hearing of the Senate Commerce, Science and Transportation Committee and the House Science Subcommittee on Space and

Aeronautics to discuss the tragic loss of the courageous crew of the Space Shuttle *Columbia,* the ongoing investigation into this tragedy, and the implications of the loss of *Columbia* to the Nation's space exploration efforts.

This morning, eleven days after the accident, our work continues to honor the solemn pledge we've made to the astronauts' families and to the American people that we will find out what caused the loss of the *Columbia* and its crew, correct what problems we find, and do our utmost to make sure this never happens again.

We welcome the Committee's interest in working with NASA to help determine how we can learn from this tragic accident so that we may continue advancing the Nation's research and exploration objectives in space while at the same time striving to ensure we make manned spaceflight as safe as humanly possible.

Throughout NASA's forty-five years of serving the public interest, Congress has been our partner, helping us achieve the goals outlined in NASA's congressionally authorized charter. This charter compels NASA to:

 Explore, use, and enable the development of space for human enterprise.

 Advance scientific knowledge and understanding of the Earth, the Solar System, and the Universe and use the environment of space for research.

 Research, develop, verify, and transfer advanced aeronautics, space, and related technologies.

With the support of Congress, NASA has amassed a record of significant achievements that have tangibly improved the lives of all Americans. When we have erred, you have helped us right our course.

This morning you will be asking us tough questions. That's as it should be. Believe me, none of the questions you will ask can be any tougher than those we are asking of ourselves.

I can assure you, however, that whatever determinations are reached regarding the cause of the accident, you will find that complacency is not one of them. Last year we temporarily halted Shuttle flight operations when tiny cracks were discovered in metal liners used to direct the fuel flow inside propellant lines on two different orbiters. We did not fly again until that problem was corrected. To signal our continued commitment to rewarding such diligence, we also made a point to praise David Strait, the young contractor employee who discovered the cracks. Other flight decisions made throughout the year were made with the goal of operational safety being paramount. And from working with the dedicated employees who keep the Shuttle flying safely I know they have the utmost regard for the enormity of their duty.

This week, at NASA Centers throughout the country and in the field, with the support of more than 2000 people from more than 20 federal, state and local organizations, the important work of data analysis and recovery operations is continuing. I am extremely proud of the work that is being conducted by these dedicated public servants. As President Bush said last week, "The people of NASA are being tested once again. In your grief, you are responding as your friends would have wished—with focus, professionalism, and unbroken faith in the mission of this agency. Captain Dave Brown was correct: America's space program will go on."

This morning, to help frame our discussion, I would like to review for you the significant actions NASA has taken since the morning of the accident in accord with our contingency plan. In addition to articulating notification or first response procedures, defining the roles and responsibilities of mishap response and mishap investigation teams, the plan specifies selection of persons outside of NASA to head an independent, seasoned accident investigation team.

While we did not foresee this terrible tragedy, our response has unfolded as we had planned and prepared for that contingency plan. This plan was one of the many positive outcomes from the terrible loss of the Space Shuttle *Challenger* seventeen years ago. The plan is updated before every flight and a contingency was simulated just three months ago.

First Response: Saturday February 1, 2003

When we first became aware of the a problem with STS–107, I was waiting at the Space Shuttle Landing Strip at the Kennedy Space Center on Saturday, February 1. At 8:59 a.m. eastern time, we lost communications with the *Columbia*.

At 9:16 a.m. the countdown arrival clock reached zero and there was no sign of the *Columbia*. Captain Bill Readdy, our Associate Administrator for Space Flight, declared a spaceflight contingency and activated the Recovery Control Center at the Kennedy Space Center. At that point, Bill Readdy and I departed the landing strip and headed to the Launch Control Center.

We arrived at the Launch Control Center thirteen minutes later, at 9:29 a.m., and we activated the Contingency Action Plan for Space Flight Operations. Through the White House Situation Room, we notified the President as well as other senior staff of the loss of communication. In addition, Members of Congress and the Government of Israel were notified. Homeland Security Secretary

Tom Ridge and the National Security Council were also made aware of the situation. Secretary Ridge then began assessing the possibility that this situation was terrorism-related. Shortly after, he made a determination that it was highly unlikely terrorism was involved.

Secretary Ridge then announced that the Federal Emergency Management Agency would be the lead federal agency for the recovery effort.

Meanwhile, the family members of the *Columbia* astronauts were escorted from the landing strip to the astronauts' crew quarters. Later that morning, at about 11:30 a.m., I met with the families at the crew quarters at Kennedy Space Center to express my condolences, offering any and all support we could give, and stated our commitment to find the cause of the accident, fix any problems we may find, and continue the work that their loved ones had started.

Data at all NASA sites and contractors were impounded at 10:00 a.m. and the Headquarters Action Center in Washington, D.C. was activated with NASA personnel moving immediately to their duty stations.

By 10:30 a.m., the NASA Mishap Response Team convened to assess the preliminary data and focus on the location of the crew compartment through the Rescue Coordination Center at Langley Air Force Base in Virginia. The Rapid Response Team was activated for deployment to Barksdale AFB in Louisiana.

Columbia Accident Investigation Board

The process of initiating the *Columbia* Accident Investigation Board began about 10:30 a.m. on Saturday, February 1, when I placed a call to NASA Deputy Administrator Fred Gregory, who was at NASA Headquarters in Washington. Mr. Gregory then began calling *Columbia* Accident Investigation Board members currently listed in our contingency plan.

At 1:15 p.m., I made a brief televised statement expressing our "deepest national regrets" for the tragic accident and informed the public about the appointment of the *Columbia* Accident Investigation Board.

I verbally activated the *Columbia* Accident Investigation Board during the NASA Mishap Investigation Team teleconference, which occurred at 5:00 p.m.

By 6:00 p.m. during a teleconference with the White House Situation Room, we briefed officials from the Department of Homeland Security, the Federal Emergency Management Agency, the Department of Defense, the FBI, and the Federal Aviation Administration about the current status of the accident investigation.

At 6:40 p.m. staff members of the National Transportation Safety Board departed Washington and traveled to Barksdale Air Force Base in Louisiana to assist as part of the Mishap Investigation Team. They were later made available to the *Columbia* Accident Investigation Board.

On Sunday, February 2, the *Columbia* Accident Investigation Board, headed by retired U.S. Navy Admiral Hal Gehman, held its first meeting at Barksdale AFB, less than 30 hours after the accident. We also began the practice of twice daily briefings at Headquarters in Washington and at the Johnson Space Center in Houston.

Membership in the *Columbia* Accident Investigation Board consists of persons selected for their positions in heading civil and military offices with responsibilities for aerospace safety accident investigations and related skills. Many have been chief investigators on major accidents and between them the *Columbia* Accident Investigation Board members have the experience of some 50 major investigations to draw upon.

Quite simply, the people who are now on the Board are some of the best in the world at what they do.

You have our assurance that this distinguished Board will be able to act with genuine independence. When the Board assembled, it modified its Charter to eliminate any reference to NASA directing the administration of the investigation. NASA accepted the changes to the Charter without objection. Further, the NASA Inspector General, Robert Cobb is an observer on the *Columbia* Accident Investigation Board and he will help assure the independence of the Board as he reports to the President and Congress.

There are some additional details about the *Columbia* Accident Investigation Board and its activities that are worth noting. The Board has taken over hardware and software releases of NASA so that NASA cannot alter anything unless the Board approves. NASA has already begun to honor document requests from the Board, and has also supplied additional documents to the Board which were not requested that we believe may be helpful to their work. And finally,. the Board has instructed NASA to conduct fault tree analysis that it intends to independently validate.

Recovery Operations

On Sunday, the NASA Mishap Investigation Team was on the ground and working with local officials in Texas and Louisiana. The State of Texas activated 800 members of the Texas National Guard to assist with the retrieval of debris.

By Tuesday, there were nearly 200 NASA and NASA contractor

personnel working recovery operations in Texas, Louisiana, Arizona, and California. They were part of the more than 2000 people from Federal Emergency Management Agency, Environmental Protection Agency, Federal Bureau of Investigation, Department of Defense, Department of Transportation, U.S. Forest Service, Texas National Guard, and state and local authorities working to locate, document, and collect debris.

By Wednesday, the astronauts' remains were transported to Dover Air Force Base in Delaware. At Dover, NASA Deputy Administrator Fred Gregory and a ceremonial honor guard were present to pay our respects to the seven fallen astronauts.

Throughout the week, we were able to make steady progress in our effort to recover debris from the accident. We have thus far recovered upwards of 12,000 elements of debris. The search effort, as you know from our press conferences, is a large, complex and ongoing effort over hundreds of square miles with challenging weather and terrain conditions. We are very grateful that no one was injured on the ground as a result of flying debris from the accident and we are working with our agency partners to ensure recovery operations remain safe.

The Federal Emergency Management Agency command post was set up in Lufkin, Texas on Saturday, February 1, and has been operating non-stop since then. Debris collection activities began at Barksdale Air Force Base on Sunday, February 2. Yesterday, we began transporting debris on trucks to the Kennedy Space Center where they will be assembled and analyzed as part of the comprehensive accident investigation directed by the Gehman Board. I visited Texas and Louisiana this past Saturday to get my own assessment of the operation and to personally thank the many volunteers who have worked so tirelessly to support the debris recovery effort.

Space Shuttle Status

Let me touch briefly on the Space Shuttle fleet as it is today. *Discovery* is continuing to undergo major inspections and upgrades which will be completed by April of 2004. *Atlantis* is currently assembled and stacked in the Vehicle Assembly Building at the Kennedy Space Center for STS–114. The *Endeavour* is in the Orbiter Processing Facility and being prepared for STS–115.

The next Shuttle mission, STS–114, was to have been to the International Space Station in March. That mission, commanded by Col. Eileen Collins, U.S. Air Force, is on hold until we understand the causes of the *Columbia* accident and are able to resolve any issues identified. At this time we don't know how long it will be before we can resume Shuttle flights. We will only know when the *Columbia* Accident Investigation Board concludes its work and presents its findings.

Columbia was the first Orbiter in the Shuttle fleet, having flown 28 successful missions or just over a quarter of its certified life of 100 flights. In February 2001, less than a year ago, *Columbia* completed a major scheduled eighteen month overhaul and update of its systems, a process we call Orbiter Major Modifications (OMM).

The STS–107 mission was *Columbia's* second flight following OMM and a successful servicing mission to the Rubble Space Telescope in March 2002.

Prior to the loss of *Columbia* and her crew, the projected Shuttle flight rate was five flights per year starting in FY 2004, and we have requested funding for that flight rate in this budget. The flight rate will be adjusted as needed once we determine when we can return to flight.

International Space Station Status

The crew of the International Space Station is of course deeply saddened by the loss of *Columbia* and her crew—as are all of our partners and people around the world. I spoke with International Space Station crew members Ken Bowersox, Don Pettit, and Nikolai Budarin on Saturday, February 1st to inform them of the accident and how we are proceeding. Despite this tragedy, the crew is continuing its busy schedule of work.

The day after the loss of STS–107, our Russian partners conducted a successful launch of an unmanned, autonomous Progress resupply vehicle to the Station. The provisions carried on Progress 10P should provide the crew sufficient supplies to maintain normal operations through June 2003.

Progress resupply flights to the International Space Station by our Russian partner will continue as scheduled. The next Progress flight is scheduled for June 8, 2003. We are working with the Russian Aviation and Space Agency officials to determine what we want to place on the flight to make sure we make the best use of the space available. In addition, a regularly scheduled Soyuz crew transport vehicle exchange is already planned for launch in April 2003.

Study teams formed almost immediately after the accident to assess the impact on the International Space Station. These teams are focused on how we will 1) sustain the Station, 2) continue to assemble the Station, and 3) maximize the utilization of this unique research platform. We have kept our International Space Station partners informed of our recovery efforts. Further, we met with our international partners last week and plan future meetings in the weeks ahead to develop an International Space Station partner plan.

We can maintain a permanent crew on the International Space Station as long as is necessary with support from Soyuz and Progress flights. The International Space Station is stable and has sufficient propellant to maintain its orbit for at least a year without support from the Space Shuttle. A nearer, term issue for crew support beyond June is water. The International Space Station cannot support a crew of three after June with the currently planned support from Progress. As a consequence, we are discussing with our international partners the possibility of changing the April Soyuz flight from a taxi mission to a crew exchange mission as well as the feasibility of adding Progress resupply flights.

I should emphasize however, that no decisions have been made and we are examining all options. I have talked to the Expedition Six crew now on-orbit and they have expressed determination and desire to do whatever is necessary to continue their research and deal with any changes in the crew rotation schedule that may be necessary.

Integrated Space Transportation Plan

As we look forward to determine our nation's best course of action in response to the *Columbia* accident, it is worth noting NASA's Integrated Space Transportation Plan (ISTP), which was submitted by the President to Congress in November as an amendment to the Fiscal Year 2003 federal budget. The Integrated Space Transportation Plan can help us address many of the near-term issues we are facing, even though it was developed prior to the loss of *Columbia*.

The Integrated Space Transportation Plan reflects the tight coupling required across the Space Station, Space Shuttle, and

Space Launch Initiatives efforts. It is intended to ensure that necessary access to the International Space Station can be supported for the foreseeable future. It consists of three major programs: the Space Shuttle, the Orbital Space Plane, and Next Generation Launch Technology.

The new plan makes investments to *extend Shuttle's operational life* for continued safe operations.

The Orbital Space Plane is designed to *provide a crew transfer capability as early as possible* to assure access to and from the International Space Station.

The Next Generation Launch Technology Program *funds next generation reusable launch vehicle technology* developments in areas such as propulsion, structures, and operations.

The SLI will focus on the Orbital Space Plane and Next Generation Launch Technology, including Third Generation RLV efforts.

The FY 2003 budget amendment also proposed adding funds to International Space Station reserves to assure that we could successfully reach the milestone of U.S. core complete and maintain progress on long-lead items for enhanced research aboard the Space Station.

Science and Research Objectives

Space flight is a means to an end and at NASA that end is research, exploration, discovery and inspiration.

The crew of STS–107 were engaged in a wide array of scientific research that could be conducted nowhere else but in space, and had significant potential benefits for the public. *Columbia's* crew took great pride in their research aimed at fighting cancer, improving crop yields, developing fire-suppression techniques, building earthquake-resistant buildings, and understanding the effects of dust storms on weather. As was written in the press, "*Columbia* had a cargo of human ingenuity."

The crew of the International Space Station is also conducting research now that can be conducted nowhere else. Thus far, more than sixty experiments spanning across such scientific disciplines as human physiology, genetics, plant biology, Earth observations, physics, and cell biology have been conducted on the International Space Station. From these experiments scientists are learning better methods of drug testing, and about dynamic models of human diseases, the physics of fundamental processes in manufacturing, antibiotic synthesis, and changes in Earth climate, vegetation, and crops.

The International Space Station is the centerpiece initiative of human space flight at NASA. Our objectives in this regard are very clear. First, we will keep our on-orbit International Space Station crew safe. Second, we intend to keep the International Space Station continuously occupied in order to assure the reliability of the International Space Station itself. Third, we intend to return to assembly as soon as we are able to return the Shuttle fleet to safe operations, and complete the research goals set for ourselves and our international partners.

To accomplish these aims, we need to create a long-term crew return capability to complement and augment the Soyuz vehicles now provided by our Russian partners. We intend to build on that new return capability to create a crew transfer system that will allow us to rotate crews on the International Space Station independently from the Space Shuttle.

We also firmly believe that extending the operational life of the remaining Shuttle fleet is a good investment because it will help maximize the science return from the International Space Station.

We designed our Integrated Space Transportation Plan (ISTP) to ensure that we had the coordinated resources to exploit the unique research environment of space and the International Space Station in the near-, mid-, and long-term.

We thought the plan was a good one when we proposed it and we believe that it is not only valid today but even more compelling to pursue. While we believe the ISTP is a good plan, we will re-examine it if necessary in light of investigation findings on *Columbia.*

Moving Forward

Just over a week ago—although it seems more like a lifetime—the President spoke eloquently and powerfully at the Johnson Space Center in Houston, Texas. He said:

"The cause of exploration and discovery is not an option we choose; it is a desire written in the human heart. We are that part of creation which seeks to understand all creation. We find the best among us, send them forth into unmapped darkness, and pray they will return. They go in peace for all mankind, and all mankind is in their debt."

The noble purposes described in President Bush's words frames all that we do and how we do it. These purposes drive our mission goals, which are:

To understand and protect our home planet; To explore the Universe and search for life; and, To inspire the next generation of explorers as only NASA can.

And even while our nonstop work to recover from this terrible tragedy and to continue safe operations on the International Space Station will be our chief focus in the days ahead, the American people should know that we will also press ahead with our other activities to achieve these important goals.

This Centennial of Flight year we will be launching the Mars Exploration Rovers, the Mars Express spacecraft, the Space InfraRed Telescope Facility, and a number of Earth Science spacecraft and instruments, as well as continuing our work to help improve aviation security on behalf of our Homeland Defense.

In these activities and in all we do at NASA, we strive for unmatched excellence. And when it comes to human space exploration, where margins are razor thin, we know we are graded on a very harsh curve. For us, ninety-six percent to ninety-nine percent is not an "A." One hundred percent is the minimum passing grade.

Despite this harsh truth, we know the lesson from this terrible accident is not to turn our backs on exploration simply because it is hard or risky. As John Shedd wrote about the age of ocean exploration, "A ship in harbor is safe, but that is not what ships are built for." Human history teaches us that in exploration, after accidents like this occur, we can learn from them and further reduce risk, although we must honestly admit that risks can never be eliminated. And as President John F. Kennedy said some 41 years ago, speaking about our fledgling space program, **"All great and honorable actions are accompanied with great difficulties, and both must be enterprised and overcome with answerable courage."**

The immediate task before the Agency is clear. We will find the problem that caused the loss of *Columbia* and its crew, we will fix it, and we will return to flight operations that are as safe as humanly possible in pursuit of knowledge. We have no preconceptions about what the cause of failure was or what it will take to make sure it never happens again. We have an independent accident investigation board of truly outstanding and eminently qualified individuals and they, and they alone, will determine the cause of the accident and its remedy—no matter where it leads.

We are ready and willing to support the addition of any experts that Admiral Gehman deems necessary to the effective conduct of the Board's investigations.

Part of my job as Administrator is to remind everyone of what NASA does and what we are capable of doing. It's a responsibility I take very seriously. At the same time that I am saddened beyond words for the loss of the seven outstanding men and women of STS–107, I am also very proud and humbled by the focus, dedication and professionalism of the NASA family and all those throughout the country who are assisting us in the recovery effort.

Today, February 12, is also the birthday of President Lincoln. And some of his words, spoken for a very different purpose, have come to be in my mind this past week:

"It is rather for us to be here dedicated to the great task remaining before us—that from these honored dead we take increased devotion to that cause for which they gave the last full measure of devotion."

We have an opportunity here and now to learn from this loss, and renew the boundless spirit of exploration present at NASA's beginning. We will do this by being accountable to the American people for our failings and, we hope, credible and compelling in pursuit of research, exploration, and inspiration for future generations.

Finally, during the 16-day STS–107 mission we had no indications that would suggest a compromise to flight safety. The time it took me to present this testimony is about the same amount of time that transpired between when Mission Control first noticed anomalies in temperature measurements and the accident.

I just paused for a few seconds. That's the same amount of time that transpired from Mission Control's last communication with the crew and our loss of signal with the heroic *Columbia* astronauts.

May God bless the crew of STS–107.

Chairman **BOEHLERT.** Thank you very much, Mr. Administrator.

The Chair recognizes the Ranking Member of the House Science Committee, the gentleman from Texas, Mr. Hall.

STATEMENT OF HON. RALPH M. HALL, U.S. REPRESENTATIVE FROM TEXAS

Representative **HALL.** Thank you, Mr. Chairman, and thank you, Chairman McCain, and I thank this group.

Mr. O'Keefe, I thank you, your Deputy and your Associate Administrator for Space Flight and those valiant people who sit behind you there that contribute so much day in and day out. We're grateful to you.

And I speak for Bart Gordon, who is the Ranking Member of the Space Subcommittee, who has the same respect I have for the leadership. And this is a day and time when we should be neither Republicans nor Democrats, but Americans. And I think it's a day in time when we come together.

And, Mr. Administrator, you did a great job that Monday, that fateful Monday, in Houston. Thank you for that.

I think, certainly, that this one of the most painful hearings that I've ever had the duty to try to get prepared for. It's less than two weeks now since the Shuttle broke apart in the sky up over my home in my area in Texas. I'm saddened every time I think of these seven brave astronauts and the grief-stricken families that they left behind. I knew three of them very well.

And the young lady from India, who had accomplished so much and came so far, came to my district on more than one occasion, had a great sense of humor, was really great for the program. In one of her speeches to one of the classes in Canton, in Vanzant, Texas, one of the students said, "We have a hard time pronouncing your name." She said, "That's all right. I have a hard time pronouncing yours."

(Laughter.)

Representative **HALL.** She had a way with youngsters and was very helpful.

I know that there are a lot of questions about what went wrong, and I'm going to shorten my speech here because we have so many others that really should be heard from and we have questions that we have to ask you.

There has also been a lot of speculation as to what or who may be to blame for the accident. The reality is that it doesn't appear that anyone yet knows what caused the accident, although the NASA Administrator may have some information in the progress of the investigation to share with us here today. And you've done that, and I thank you. And I think the questions will elicit more information and will be helpful to us.

So it might be some time before we'll be clear on what factors have contributed to the accident. Thus, it's important that we have a thorough and, I want to stress, independent, as Mr. Gordon has stressed, investigation of the accident so that the American people can be assured that everything's on top of the table. And I know that's what everybody in this room wants. Anything less would be a disservice to the courageous men and women who died on the *Columbia.*

Our nation is grieving. We're mournful at this time. And the families are in mourning. But time lessens and sometimes heals that. But that same time is going to bolster the need for an independent investigation, and that's what we're looking for. And, Mr. Administrator, I understand that you've pledged to do that, and we thank you for that.

I think we need to take a very close look at what can be done to improve Shuttle crew survivability. As a long-time Member of this committee, I've always had problems cutting the NASA budget, because not having the knowledge that you men have, not having the exposure of life or death that so many of you have, I didn't know how to cut it or how to recommend cutting it without endangering someone. So we've had to call on the Administrator to do that. We had to call on Dan Goldin to do that. He did it, and, I think, did it in a good manner. We call on you, Mr. O'Keefe, to give us that same type leadership, and we pledge our support to you as we seek out causation and how to keep it from ever happening again.

NASA's talking about spending upwards of $9 to $13 billion, by its own estimates, over the next decade to develop a still-to-be-defined Orbital Space Plane. That's long-range planning. We have to have that, and we have to have some short-range decisions.

I think we need to examine whether some of that money would be better spent on developing crew escape systems for the existing Shuttle fleet and on completing a simply, reliable U.S. crew rescue vehicle for the International Space Station, and doing both of these things as soon as possible.

With that, Mr. Chairman, I'd like unanimous consent to put my full speech in the record, and I yield back the time.

Thank you.

Chairman **MCCAIN.** Without objection.

[The prepared statement of Mr. Hall follows:]

PREPARED STATEMENT OF REPRESENTATIVE RALPH M. HALL

This is one of the most painful hearings that I have had to prepare for in all my years in Congress. It is now less than two weeks since the Space Shuttle *Columbia* broke apart in the sky over my home state of Texas. I'm saddened every time I think of those seven brave astronauts and the grief-stricken families and friends that they left behind. They made the ultimate sacrifice for the cause of space exploration, and we shall miss them dearly.

When the STS–107 mission was launched into orbit in mid-January, I was looking forward to what we would learn from it. As many of you know, it was a mission dedicated to research. As a result, it was a mission that offered the promise of improving the lives of our citizens back here on Earth. That is the vision I have long had for our space program: learning things in space that can be used for the benefit of all Americans. It is what the International Space Station should be about if this nation will step up and honor our long-standing commitments to complete the project. And it is what the astronauts of STS–107 were trying to accomplish on their ill-fated mission.

I know that there are many questions about what went wrong. There has also been a lot of speculation as to what or who may be to blame for the accident. The reality is that it doesn't appear that anyone yet knows what caused the accident, although the NASA Administrator may have some information on the progress of the investigation to share with us today. So it's likely to be some time before we can be clear on what factor, may have contributed to the accident. It thus is important that we have a thorough, independent investigation of the accident so that the American people can be assured that nothing is being hidden. Anything less would be a disservice to the courageous men and women who died on *Columbia.*

Whatever the specific cause of the *Columbia* accident, we in Congress need to take a hard look at where we go from here. NASA's latest proposal doesn't envision having an alternative means of launching crews into space for another decade or more. And in any event, NASA seems to lie committed to flying the Shuttle to the Space Station throughout the lifetime of the Station. A decade or more is a long time. If, God forbid, there is another accident sometime during that decade, will we be able to look back and say we had done all we could to improve the crew's chances of survival? I hope so.

For example, the Aerospace Safety Advisory Panel's March 2002 report found that *17 years* after the *Challenger* accident the Shuttle program still is facing a situation where:

"there is no in-flight crew escape system for the Orbiter other than for abort below 20,000 feet during a controlled glide"

and it recommended that NASA:

"complete the ongoing studies of crew escape design options and implement an improved system as soon as possible."

I think we need to take a close look at what could be done to improve Shuttle crew survivability. NASA is talking about spending upwards of $9 to $13 billion by its own estimates over the next decade to develop a still-to-be-defined Orbital Space Plane. I think we need to examine whether some of that money would be better spent on developing crew escape systems for the existing Shuttle fleet and on completing a simple, reliable U.S. crew rescue vehicle for the International Space Station—and doing both of those things as soon as possible. I don't think the brave men and women who serve in our nation's space program should be needlessly put into harm's way any longer than necessary if there are practical remedies available.

Thank you, and I yield back the balance of my time.

Chairman **MCCAIN.** Senator Stevens has to return quickly to chair the conference concerning the Omnibus Appropriations bill, which all of us eagerly await the result of his work, and so he'd like to make a brief statement.

Senator Stevens.

STATEMENT OF HON. TED STEVENS, U.S. SENATOR FROM ALASKA

Senator **STEVENS.** Mr. Chairman, I thank you, and I do have to return to that conference. I have come because the gentleman that's before you I consider to be one of the closest friends I have in the world. I think members should know who he is.

He came to Washington as a White House fellow. He worked for the Department of Navy, and then he became a Senate employee and became the chief of staff of the Defense Appropriations Subcommittee. He went from there to become the Comptroller of the Department of Defense, the Secretary of the Navy. He subsequently became a professor at Syracuse University, then a deputy director of the Office of Management Budget, and is now the administrator of NASA.

I know of no one who has committed himself to good government and conducted himself in the finest of our traditions than Sean O'Keefe. He is a man of integrity, of complete honest and openness in all he does. I would back him, as I know he would me, with my life. And I urge you to listen to Sean O'Keefe today. He'll tell you the truth.

Thank you very much.

Mr. **O'KEEFE.** Thank you, Senator.

Chairman **MCCAIN.** Thank you very much, Senator Stevens.

Discussion

Effects of Budget Decisions on Shuttle Program

Thank you, Mr. O'Keefe, for your presentation.

Look, one of the issues that is going to be talked about a lot today by a lot of the members is the issue as to whether the NASA's budget was, "starved," cut to the bone. There will be allegations that certain recommendations were made by certain people.

For example, the Aerospace Safety Advisory Panel annual report for 2001 stated, "The current and proposed budget are not sufficient to improve or even maintain the safety risk level of operating the Space Shuttle." I've seen a lot of rhetoric in the media, and you have too, that you were "starved." That was not my experience, as Chairman and Ranking Member of the Commerce Committee, but I think it's very important that you take that issue head on and immediately.

Mr. **O'KEEFE.** Yes, sir. No, I fully agree. There is no question, this is a concern that we continue to have, as well, and to assure that all of the facts that are laid out on that particular matter. As it pertains the views of the ASAP and the advisory committee, as well, their reports, I think, reiterate consistently their view that the future concerns about Space Shuttle operations and safety considerations were the matter they were most focused on. As a consequence, their continued effort that I see in the report before us always is that they quote specifically, "It's important to stress that the panel believes that safety has not yet been compromised. NASA and its contractors maintain excellent safety practices and processes, as well as an appropriate level of safety consciousness. This has been—contributed to significant flight achievements in the defined requirements for operating, and an acceptable level of risk are always met."

So their concerns were always presented in the context of future approaches. And, as a matter of fact, if we call up slide number 35, that will cover that particular question, as well. Their focus was always on the future operations as well as future efforts that were to be engaged in.

At the present time, in terms of current operations and activities they certified as recently as a year ago, they felt that the current operations were concentrated on very specifically to assure flight safety as a primary paramount objective.

Chairman **MCCAIN.** I think you're going to be confronted with some numbers in further questioning, and I hope you will have responses to that, as well.

At a Commerce Committee September 6th, 2001, hearing on Shuttle safety, William Readdy, then Deputy Associate Administrator of the Office of Space Flight, acknowledged the challenges NASA was facing to maintain Shuttle safety in light of budgetary constraints, but, nevertheless, stated, "The safety of the Space Shuttle has also been dramatically improved by reducing risk by more than a factor of five." Later in his testimony, he said, quote, "The Space Shuttle is the safest, most capable and reliable transportation system in the world."

Mr. Blomberg, the former chief of NASA's Aerospace Safety Advisory Panel, testifying before the House Science Committee in April 2002 on behalf of the advisory panel, stated that, quote, "In all the years of my involvement, I have never been as concerned for Space Shuttle safety as I am right now. The concern is not for the present flight or the next or perhaps the one after that. In fact, one of the roots of my concern is that nobody will know for sure when the safety margins have been eroded too far. All of my instincts, however, suggest that the current approach is planting the seeds for future danger."

How do we reconcile those two statements by two highly regarded individuals who are within the bureaucracy of NASA?

Mr. **O'KEEFE.** Yes, sir. Well, just to clarify the record on that, Bill Readdy, of course, is the Associate Administrator for Space Flight. Richard Blomberg was a independent external member of and a chairman of the advisory panel for safety, so he was not a full-time NASA employee in that regard. He was representing a panel view.

Reconciling that is—I think if you trace the history just a little bit, the plan that had existed until this past November contemplated the retirement of the Space Shuttle fleet as early as the middle of this decade, certainly no later than 2012, so it altered over the course of several years from about '95 forward, the best I can tell, over the history of this.

Based on the recommendations of that advisory panel on safety, as well as the testimony and comments made at several different committee hearings, as well, we went back and really looked seriously at the question of what it would take in order to maintain Shuttle operations for a sustained period of time, what kind of continued upgrades would be necessary, modifications necessary, in order to assure safe flight operations, and on the basis of that, as recently as last summer, went through that planning effort, which ultimately yielded the amendment that was sent forward by the President on November 13th of last year to propose a specific change in the funding profile for Shuttle, which envisioned a maintenance of that asset for a sustained period of time, though next decade.

So the focus of these concerns, which were all exactly as you stated, Mr. Chairman, in context of future concern, were the things we were very mindful of, took heed of, made adjustments to, and specifically put in plan in order to assure that we covered those kinds of concerns in the future and addressed those.

As it pertained to current flight operations, again there was no indication that I knew of that raised concerns along the way of current flight operations. If anything, the diligence that I see among the entire folk in NASA, in the community, is very much that of a culture that's dedicated to assuring safe flight operations, or else the launch doesn't occur. And that is the mindset and ethos we continue to encourage and will continue to encourage in the future.

Changes Needed to Assure an Independent Investigation

Chairman **BOEHLERT.** Mr. O'Keefe, as I mentioned in my opening statement, I remain concerned about language throughout the charter of the *Columbia* Accident Investigation Board. The language would appear to indicate that everything the board does is subject to NASA approval, and that, to me, raises some fundamental questions about the independence of the board. And we all want the board to be independent, and not just in name, but in fact.

Are you willing to re-examine that charter and remove some of the language that raises these questions and make adjustments in other places?

Mr. **O'KEEFE.** Yes, sir. We'll continue to work with Admiral Gehman to assure whatever he needs in order to guarantee the independence and objectivity of that board. We will absolutely work with him, without objection.

Chairman **BOEHLERT.** I mean, just to give you an example, the independent board will conduct activities in accordance with the provisions of applicable NASA policies and procedures. And then it goes on to say, "The interim scheduled board activities, interim board reports, and the submission of final board report, in coordination with the NASA Administrator." I would think that they would have independence, they could schedule their meetings and determine the type of report they want to submit. Of course they will submit the report to you. But the report should come also to the—the final report—not just to the NASA administrator, but to the President, the Congress, and the American people. So I think that charter has to be revisited, and very promptly.

We've already had conversations with each other, and I have had with Admiral Gehman, and both have assured me that additional members from outside the community, so to speak, and experts in different fields, will be added to the board. I think that's very important.

It's essential that we maintain the independent nature of the board.

Mr. **O'KEEFE.** I fully concur, Mr. Chairman. And, as a matter of fact, I think in Admiral Gehman's press conference yesterday, he was very explicit that all of the factors he needed in order to maintain independence and to be an objective investigator in this particular case, for all of his board members, was what the present condition required.

Having said that, if, on examination, the latest change that was made to the charter at his request, we made it, if he wants further changes they'll be made, as well, anything that it takes in order to guarantee their independence, because we will be guided by their findings. And, as I've reiterated publicly as well as to you, sir, and to him, that about the only thing that will be unique about the reporting requirement is that he'll be putting an address that says NASA on it, on the envelope, sending it to us. But that report will be made public concurrent with its receipt. So he will be reporting to the President, to the Congress, to the American people, to all of us simultaneously.

Contractor Incentives and Obligations

Chairman **BOEHLERT.** Well, I was comforted by my conversation with Admiral Gehman, because he is insisting on independence, and he has also indicated, obviously, he'll have to have a liaison with NASA and use some of your resources, but the staffing will be independent of NASA, and I think that's essential.

Obviously, we're all going to be spending a lot of time looking at Shuttle contracts even though there's no indication at this point that they are a problem. How comfortable are you that the incentives in the current contracts captured the proper balance between efficiency and safety? And then, as a follow-on, do the contracts have clauses that will ensure that the contractors have to, must, cooperate with fully with the Gehman investigation?

Mr. **O'KEEFE.** Yes, sir. On the first part, the emphasis on safety in the current Space Flight Operations Contract that we have very much emphasizes the safety parameters. And, indeed, they have tremendous incentives to do better each and every time. And as a consequence of that, there are a series of weighted factors in the guidelines that heavily look at the metrics of any difficulties or problems on orbit or at launch or any other time. As they drive those factors down, they're given a specific incentive to do better in each of those cases. So they've got a powerful motivation to want to move in that direction.

In doing so, I think the approach also yields some efficiencies. But that's a secondary matter, at most. And so, as a result, there are real advantages and real emphasis on the safety considerations that are currently built into that contract framework.

As it pertains to their cooperation with the Gehman Board, positively we will advise them, and have, that we fully expect everyone to be cooperative with that board. We have absolutely nothing to hide. There is no evidence or no fact that we can think of out there, short of national security information or some private proprietary issue that some individual may want to assert, that would preclude us from making any information available. And so everyone within the contractor community should feel the same as we do.

Chairman **BOEHLERT.** But is there something more than a moral obligation or a desire? Is there something that binds them, commits them, to cooperate fully with the Gehman investigation board?

Mr. **O'KEEFE.** I will take you up on your opening statement that, on that contract clause, I don't know, but I'll find out.

Chairman **BOEHLERT.** Thank you very much.

Mr. **O'KEEFE.** Thank you, Mr. Chairman.

Chairman **MCCAIN.** Senator Hollings.

NASA's Budget Request to OMB

Senator **HOLLINGS.** Right to the point with respect to costs, and I'm sure you don't have, Mr. O'Keefe, the actual figures with you, but on the shortchanging of the space program, we had a report yesterday in the *New York Times* stating that we cut the space program $800 million. I've been checking it overnight. At my check, it's $700 million.

Be that as it may, what's the truth? That's what we want. Last week I asked Mitch Daniels, Director of the Office of Management and Budget, to furnish the Budget Committee the figures of what was requested by NASA. I want you to furnish the figures that were requested by NASA of OMB for the last 10 years. And not just this Administration, but the past Administrations so we can see the trend line and exactly how we financed it.

Yes, we all are trying to find out the cause. But, in the meantime, as you try to piece together the retrieved parts and everything else like that, I don't know how long that'll take, a year or months, whatever it is, we all want to see the space program continue. And for this senator, I don't want it to continue with upgrades.

I've heard enough about these upgrades. We've lost 14 astronauts and $5 billion in hardware with upgrades, and we had a new reusable launch vehicle. We had a spaceship that was cancelled the year before last. Then we had a Reusable Launch Vehicle, and that was cancelled last November, just a couple of months ago. And you said we were going to use these vehicles, Shuttles, until 2020. Are you willing to use one of these Shuttles with all of the tiles flying off? And after all of these losses, you'd still want to use them until 2020 and not get new technology, Mr. Administrator?

Mr. **O'KEEFE.** Yes, sir. No, thank you. As I understand the history here, the effort during the course of the '90's was in anticipation of a retirement of Shuttle concurrent with the introduction of a new Reusable Launch Vehicle. That was envisioned to be the X–33, as I understand it. Based on a variety of technical issues, which were based on the assumption that a series of unconquerable engineering and laws of physics challenges would be overcome, ultimately that—two-plus years ago, the choice was made to cancel that program and to continue with Shuttle operations.

What we proposed a year ago and is not a cancellation of any RLV effort, Reusable Launch Vehicle, instead it's a selection, if you will, of looking at the Integrated Space Transportation Plan.

What's included in the November amendment that the President sent forward for the 2003 budget is a selection specifically of an Orbital Space Plane option which, frankly, is not a technology leap. It is the capability of putting aboard an Expendable Launch Vehicle, a orbital space system, space plane, that would be launched in a conventional manner using an Expendable Launch Vehicle.

The next generation beyond that is what we focus on our Next-Generation Launch Technology. So we've tried to narrow and focus a lot more the Space Launch Initiative efforts in order to get some near-term gain to supplement, to complement, the Space Shuttle and to provide that dynamic as well as flexible return system and transfer system to the International Space System and also to pursue the development of a Reusable Launch Vehicle that may be, hopefully, the product of breakthroughs that were not possible that forced the motivation or the cancellation a few years ago of the X–33.

So we're trying to do both of those concurrently, but to get some near-term capability, and, in the meantime, use Shuttle in the future as a cargo lift, heavy lift capacity, which is what it was really designed to do in the first place, rather than a crew transfer capability. So we're trying to balance both ends of that to utilize capabilities for their best purposes as we move along.

Senator **HOLLINGS.** We've got to find out what you think we ought to Appropriate. We all want to continue space exploration, but we just don't want to waste time waiting on the results, on the one hand, and trying to find out what we already know. Let's get on and get your best advice on how we should proceed to get going on this thing, and not just with upgrades.

Mr. **O'KEEFE.** Yes, sir. No, the——

Chairman **BOEHLERT.** Thank you very much, Senator.

Mr. Hall.

Crew Escape Systems

Representative **HALL.** Mr. O'Keefe, you heard my opening statement. And I'm, quite frankly, disappointed that 17 years after the *Challenger* accident so little attention has been given to developing crew escape systems for our astronauts, whether they're flying on the Shuttle or whether they're in the space station. I know you share that.

I share with you the disappointment and the blame—I've been here 23 years, so it's a partnership for us, and that's what it is, that's what it'll continue to be, but especially since NASA has indicated that the Shuttle is going to fly for another decade and a half, and maybe, probably, longer than that, and in light of a media report, I think on February the 5th, that NASA's most recent effort in that regard was a $5 million so-called "study" in 2001.

To put that study in context, the amount expended on that study of potential a Shuttle crew escape system amounted to just a little bit more than one-tenth of one percent of a single year's budget. That doesn't strike me as being very aggressive in your effort to look for ways to improve the odds of survival for astronauts in the event of a Shuttle accident.

That leads me to say that I have no doubt that it's going to be challenging to develop practical crew escape systems for the Shuttle, but NASA is in the business of performing miracles, NASA is in the business of meeting challenges, and we call on you to do that.

I'm very afraid that a clue as to why NASA has not done more is found elsewhere in that article, namely, and I quote, "The proposed fixes were also seen as prohibitively expensive additions to an already aging and financially strapped Shuttle fleet." We've seen a similar situation with regard to developing a Crew Rescue Vehicle for the International Space Station.

So, as you know, NASA decided to cancel the ongoing development of U.S. Crew Rescue Vehicles, just a demonstration vehicle, we thought was nearing its flight test. And now we're dependent on the Russians for their Crew Rescue Vehicles until the end of this decade.

So, in the meantime, I guess my question to you is, Did you explicitly consider investing in the development of Space Shuttle crew escape systems when you revised the Integrated Space Transportation Plan that you announced last November?

Mr. **O'KEEFE.** Yes, sir. We're continuing to look at what we would use as enhancements, if you will, of the Space Shuttle as part of that November amendment that was submitted last November, and we're getting together here, had planned to all along, to identify that priority set of what will emphasize the highest safety margin improvements that could be yielded from different modifications of the orbiter system.

But with regard to the specific crew escape efforts, recall that since *Challenger* there have been a number of operational changes made. There is an egress system that was put into place right after the *Challenger* accident that was part of the Rogers Commission recommendations—that ultimately stemmed from it, I should say—that we put in to place that now still exist to this day.

Once launched, though, there is a number of different approaches that have been proposed, examined, reviewed, and all of which added significant amounts of weight, I'm advised, to the overall effort, and so, as a consequence, were viewed to be technically infeasible.

What we have instituted, though, is, again, a series of abort procedures. And, as recently as the December launch of the STS–113, on a perfectly clear night at Cape Canaveral in Florida, where everything was nominal, everything was ready to go, all the systems were completely operational, we scrubbed the launch because the alternate abort site at Zaragossa, Spain, the weather continued to be marginal. So we take every precaution in this process in order to assure that, all the way through assent, that every possible opportunity is there as much as possible.

But, again, the idea of an escape system was looked at, examined very thoroughly, and the conclusion was that the weight factor would almost be prohibitive in terms of its technical clarification.

So we'll continue to look at that. We'll go back and look at it again, you bet. In light of this circumstance, we really do need to focus entirely on what all the alternatives are, and I guarantee you, sir, we'll make that part of our effort underway now as part of this November amendment that is before the Congress to consider for the 2003 program, that we'll factor that into the equation and proceed as appropriate.

Representative **HALL.** Even on a local level, city councils rarely ever fix a bad bridge or a bad turn in the road until a teenager gets killed, and then it's too late. It seems to me that we launched the vehicle without any ability to dock. We lost the vehicle because we didn't have telescopic ability to inspect. We have three birds left. I just urge caution. And I thank you for your time.

I yield back my time.

Mr. **O'KEEFE.** Thank you, Congressman. I appreciate it very much.

Chairman **MCCAIN.** Senator Brownback.

Questioning NASA's Goals and Objectives

Senator **BROWNBACK.** Thank you very much, Mr. Chairman. And, Mr. O'Keefe, thank you very much for coming in front of our Joint Committees here and your great leadership at NASA in a very difficult and trying and challenging time.

We all grieve the loss of human life that's happened to NASA And at this particular point, I'm chairing a subcommittee in the Senate that'll be dealing with this, and I want to work with you and your agency as we lay out the future of manned space flight in the United States.

I want to ask you about the broad objectives and broad program objectives that we're talking about right now. It seems to me that the space program is really at a critical juncture and that the totality of the space program is. And it's got to decide amongst a couple of competing options. One is to maintain the current set of programs and current missions. The second one that you read a lot about in the newspaper and people speculate is to dramatically reduce manned space flight, go into more robotics and different types of vehicles, questioning about the safety and to try to be more safe.

And the third, a number of people are saying that our vision is too small in space currently right now, that we need new initiatives, we need to go back to the Moon, we need to go to Mars. And we're at this tremendous fork-in-the-road decision of which path to take.

It's certainly my intent in the Subcommittee to look closely at where NASA has been and where you are today and where we plan to go into the future. And, most importantly, we need to discuss, as well, the financial situation, the terms of how we get NASA where it needs to be. I'm glad to see that, in the Appropriations Committee, we're putting in an additional $414 million over the President's request.

The goal is to reflect an accurate and effective determination for the future of NASA, and I would simply like to ask you, What have you done recently—and I realize you're dealing with the tragedy mostly now, but—to look at this need for a review of the mission of NASA amongst these three policy objectives, have you had a chance to start contemplating some of that? And I hope you'll be open to working openly with the Congress as we look at this fork in the road we're in right now.

Mr. **O'KEEFE.** Yes, sir. Of course, Senator, I'd be delighted to work with you and any other Members of Congress to sort through really what is the proper role and objective of NASA in our pursuit of exploration objectives, always.

We have, indeed, had an opportunity prior to February 1st to really think seriously about what is the strategy and the focus of how we concentrate on what we do best, and do that only in a way that guarantees and assures that we—to offer to folks that we can actually deliver on and have a capability to look at longer-term exploration objectives. And I think that's contained in the strategic planning documents that were all forwarded, along with the budget that was submitted by the President just last Monday.

Prior to that, in all the efforts we put into it, was to think seriously about the very kind of questions you've raised, and, again, to narrowly focus on the kinds of exploration and discovery objectives we think we do exceptionally well. And, for those that are done by others or can be pursued elsewhere, to leave that to folks who have expertise or capabilities that would otherwise have to be duplicated by us.

What it leads to, I think, is a stepping-stone approach, an exploration strategy, if you will, that assumes that we start off with a series of robotic capabilities, and moves forward then, thereafter, toward other exploration objectives that may or may not involve human involvement.

The best example that we've seen played before us in the last several years is the Hubble Space Telescope. There was a $2 billion capability that, when launched in 1992, in fairly short order was deemed to be, as a marvelous robotic capacity, a capability that was in need of an eye examination, if you will, a lense correction. And it was, at that time, determined to be a $2 billion piece of space junk. A year later, we were able to send a Shuttle flight with astronomers and other engineering capability that was resonant among the astronauts there to make that correction. That could not have been done remotely.

And so the human intervention that was necessary to adjust that, and all the servicing missions we've done since that time, have yielded the kind of astronomy breakthroughs and discovery, just in this past year, that we never dreamed imaginable. So that combination, that heel-toe kind of approach towards a strategy that utilizes robotic capabilities, much like we're going to do here in the coming months when we send the Mars explorers in May and June of this year intended for landing in January of '04, is to then consider all the efforts we've got to do to prepare for, then, the follow-on kinds of exploration objectives.

But, again, the reiteration of the first commitment to you, positively we'll continue to work together and refine this strategy to assure that we do it with least risk, but the greatest opportunity for exploration and discovery potential.

Senator **BROWNBACK.** Thank you. And I look forward to working with you on that design of where we——

Chairman **MCCAIN.** The gentleman's time has expired.

Mr. **O'KEEFE.** Thank you, Senator.

Chairman **BOEHLERT.** Mr. Rohrabacher.

Representative **ROHRABACHER.** Thank you very much.

First and foremost, I'd like to associate myself with the remarks and the concerns of Chairman Boehlert about the basic nature and the importance of the integrity of this commission's investigation and our oversight of that commission's work.

Second of all, I would like to just note that, at the memorial service down in Texas I was touched particularly by the people of Texas, and especially by the children of Texas, who, as we went to this memorial service, they came out on the streets and roads and waved little American flags and had little signs up to encourage us, and it was very encouraging for our country. So we recognize that there was a special bond between the children of America and our astronauts.

And today we're building, and we're going to make sure that we build a better future for our children. And if there's going to be a better future for our children, we've got to have a viable space program that will keep them in the forefront of this great human endeavor of going into space and pioneering space.

So let me—I have a few thoughts, and I'll have a few questions for you. The hardworking and patriotic people of NASA have always understood and appreciated the risks with space exploration, especially manned missions. Unfortunately, in the past 17 years, we have been reminded of the dangers of human space flight with the destruction of the Space Shuttle *Challenger* in 1996—or '86, I should say —and now the *Columbia*.

Seventeen years ago, we took a step backwards for a few moments to take a look at that tragedy and pinpoint to our satisfaction what caused it and then correct those causes, at least the technical causes of the loss.

Today, I am confident that Admiral Gehman and his commission will get to the truths that will help us understand *Columbia*'s fatal accident. However, many questions need to be addressed that transcend the immediate technical and managerial problems of this tragedy.

We're going to hear a lot about the technical end of it, but there's a lot of other questions that go way beyond that. The lack of long-term goals or a unifying vision for America's space effort, for example, needs to be addressed to fully understand this tragedy. This failing, I believe, weaken the efforts that would have been taken to replace the Shuttle system long before age became a factor. And we will find out, I believe, that age was, indeed, a factor.

Perhaps Mr. Hollings, or Senator Hollings, is right, perhaps it's simple what we're looking at. Perhaps it was the tiles and—in terms of a simple answer; and a more complex answer might be facing—it might be age. But this tragedy and this investigation, nonetheless, gives us an opportunity to revisit the fundamentals and make recommendations that will chart America's future space endeavors.

NASA's leadership has faced, and will continue to face, the challenge of exercising responsible stewardship with limited resources while providing a coherent blueprint of what can be accomplished and how it can be accomplished. But hopefully, forward-looking strategies will lead us to incremental advances that will then permit us to achieve long-term objectives. A new propulsion system might be a good start, as well as, perhaps, a look at robotics and remote control on the part of NASA, a new commitment on that end. But before we move forward, we must fully understand why these seven people perished.

My question to you today is, the age factor, Was this Shuttle's age, a 30-year-old system, a major factor in this tragedy we're investigating today?

Chairman **BOEHLERT**. Administrator O'Keefe.

Mr. **O'KEEFE**. Well, thank you, Congressman. And, again, I associate myself entirely with your observation that ultimately the investigation will be what guides us to that conclusion. And if that is a factor, you bet, that's exactly what we'll operate on.

Having said that, it is worth noting two really important factors on this. The *Columbia*, indeed, is the oldest, or was the oldest, of the four orbiters. It was delivered in late 1970's. Its first flight was in 1981. It was half the age of the average bomber aircraft that flew in Afghanistan just a year ago that prosecuted that very important effort that we were engaged in there.

So the air frame condition on this—each time we go through this orbiter major modification I referred to in the opening statement— is essentially the equivalent of the same kind of effort the military, the Defense Department, goes through of tear-down of every single element of the capability of the orbiter itself, its structural integrity inspected and examined very carefully, then rebuilt to modernize it to contemporary capability. That particular effort had just been conducted, an 18-month tear-down of the Shuttle *Columbia*, and delivered early last year in advance of the March flight that went to Hubble, that did the servicing mission. STS–109 was the first flight of *Columbia* after that particular Orbiter Major Modification effort, which, again, is patterned very much after the depot kind of approach that's taken at all of the Defense Department-related assets, only even more exhaustively to conduct the upgrades. This was the second flight after that particular tear-down.

So the age factor, again, you're exactly right, the investigation may yet prove or may demonstrate to us that there was a contributor there. But in terms of our efforts to assure that not be a factor, again, it appears to be every element of diligence could be done to assure that, there was a previous flight that operated just perfectly, no difficulty whatsoever on *Columbia*, no structural defects upon return. And upon every single orbiter flight return, we examine all of the elements of the Shuttles themselves, the orbiters themselves, and we move it through the Orbiter Processing Facility to assure that any damage, any structural problems, anything are detected. And there was absolutely nothing wrong with the *Columbia* that we could detect in that regard. So when it flew on its second flight, it was in the same shape it was when it left the Orbiter Major Modification program just a year before.

History of Tile Damage and Loss

Chairman **MCCAIN.** Senator Breaux.

Senator **BREAUX.** Thank you, Mr. Chairman.

Mr. O'Keefe, thank you. I want to also congratulate you on the method in which you've handled this tragedy and the openness that I think we've seen from NASA in how you are approaching the investigation, both internally and with the external investigation, as well.

Let me ask, do we have any idea of how many times the insulating tiles have come off a Shuttle during launch and how many tiles have actually come off during the history of the Shuttle launches?

Mr. **O'KEEFE.** To the best of my recollection, sir, in our efforts there, it's no more than a half a dozen times that was specifically related to it. After each flight, there is always, again, as I mentioned just a moment ago to Congressman Rohrabacher, an assessment summary that's conducted to look at each element of the orbiter when it returns. There's also an inspection of the external tank, which, as you're aware, when it reaches the upper atmosphere, it disintegrates. The two Solid Rocket Boosters, once expended, drop back into the ocean——

Senator **BREAUX.** Well, but on the tiles themselves.

Mr. **O'KEEFE.** I'm sorry.

Senator **BREAUX.** How many times have the tiles come off, and how many tiles have come off during the history of the Shuttle launches?

Mr. **O'KEEFE.** Yes, sir. At each flight, there's typically a ding or a scratch or whatever else from all the various efforts that occur as they are re-entering, as well as on ascent. I'll provide, for the record, a full summary of all of the times on each flight that a tile has been missing or lost or whatever else. But it was never considered to be significant, in terms of its safety-of-flight consideration that we've examined on the orbiters when we moved it through the Orbiter Processing Facility to look at the condition of the orbiters after each flight. But we'll submit that for the record, sir.

Senator **BREAUX.** If engineers on this particular case had determined that insulating tiles had, in fact, departed the Shuttle at some point and that it was in an area that was important and very key, could the angle of attack on the re-entry of the Shuttle have been adjusted to deflect the heat?

Mr. **O'KEEFE.** That's a potential maneuvering capability. But, again, there are more than 4,000 sensors aboard each Shuttle orbiter, and if there were any indication that there were any abnormalities as a consequence of tile loss or whatever else, they likely would have shown up during that 16-day orbiting mission.

More importantly, during the course of that time, recall that in each orbit you're looking at a sunset and a sunrise every 90 minutes, which means every 16 times a day, the temperature variation on an orbiter or a Shuttle flight varies by as much as three to four hundred degrees, plus—200 degrees during the sunlight, and minus about 150-plus during the darkness period of that 90-degree rotation—or 90-minute rotation each time it orbits. So that wide range of temperature variation, if there had been exposure, almost certainly would have shown up on one of those 4,000 sensors that are aboard the Shuttle orbiter to have given us an indication.

The fact of the matter remains, there were no abnormalities that would suggest that problem until 8:53 the morning of Saturday, February the 1st.

Senator **BREAUX.** But is there no way that these sensors or any other methodology would have determined if any of the tiles had departed the Shuttle during the actual mission, before it returned to Earth?

Mr. **O'KEEFE.** We don't think so. Every effort that were made on previous flights to examine any structural damage or change or whatever else using any kind of visual capabilities were either inconclusive or not of the level of granularity that really gave us that much detail. And, again, all the supporting data would have also suggested if there were problems on it.

Again, the reality remains, over that 16-day mission—and, again, the investigation may find some data that we're not aware of right now, because everything was locked down within a half an hour after the incident. If there's something else that emerges to suggest to the contrary, we're going to get to the bottom of it. But all the information we have now and after the flight and after the examination of it, suggests no abnormalities that would have pointed in that direction at all.

Senator **BREAUX.** What degree of certainty——

Chairman **MCCAIN.** The gentleman's time has expired.

Chairman **BOEHLERT.** Mr. Gordon.

Reiterating the Need for an Independent Investigation Board

Representative **GORDON.** Thank you, Mr. Chairman. And welcome, Mr. O'Keefe. I'm glad you joined us today.

Before I move to discuss other issues, I just want to stress my concern that the investigation of the *Columbia* Space Shuttle accident ultimately must be perceived as objective and independent if Congress, the President, and the American taxpayers are going to reach a consensus on how to move forward with our space program. It's no reflection on you or the Admiral, but that's not going to be possible if there are lingering questions regarding the independence of the board.

As you know, I've raised this question for several days now. And having checked with your office this week and the NASA Web site this morning, there seems to be a clear disconnect from your statements about the board's independence and the rules you're laying down for the board.

Let me quote just a few examples of your rules, as Mr. Boehlert had earlier. The current board not only includes NASA employees, but you also require it to be staffed by NASA employees who will help write the board's final report, which goes to you. You require that the board must, and I quote, "schedule board activities, interim board reports, and submit the final board report in coordination with the NASA administrator in accordance with the applicable NASA policies."

Now, Mr. O'Keefe, I am afraid this will not pass anybody's smell test of independence. So please, let us move forward in a concrete way and put this bipartisan concern behind us.

ASAP's Safety Concerns

Now, let me turn to another issue that is troubling. As you know, there have been numerous warning flags regarding the health of the Shuttle program in recent years. Just a few examples. April 2002, Richard Blomberg, head of the Independent Aerospace Safety Advisory Panel, issued a blunt warning when he testified before this House Subcommittee. And I quote, "In all the years of my involvement, I have never been as concerned for the Space Shuttle safety as I am now."

A month earlier, the Aerospace Safety Advisory Panel gave you a report that stated, and I quote, "The current and proposed budgets are not sufficient to improve or even maintain the safety risk level of operations for the Space Shuttle."

Yet in spite of these warnings, you sent over a NASA budget request that cut the budget for Shuttle upgrades by $500 million, even while finding a billion dollars for new initiatives.

Because of my concern, I asked Fred Gregory, who was then the NASA Associate Administration for Space Flight, the following question at this same April 2002 hearing. "Mr. Gregory, how would you support the space station in the event you lost a Shuttle and the rest of the fleet was grounded for some period of time?" Mr. Gregory responded, "There would be no way to do that."

Now, I assumed that such an admission would have kicked off an intense effort to develop a contingency plan for supporting the space station. However, at your press briefing Monday, you indicated that over the next few weeks NASA would be working with the space station international partners to come up with a plan. You reiterated that earlier today.

Given the fact that you've had numerous warnings and you knew the Shuttle was grounded for two-and-a-half years after the loss of *Challenger,* I would assume Mr. Gregory's admission nearly a year ago would have been a wake-up call.

So my questions are, Did NASA prepare a contingency plan for the space station last year? If so, what was in the plan, and why do you now believe that you need to redo it? And, finally, if you didn't have a plan, why not?

Mr. **O'KEEFE.** Yes, sir. We did prepare a contingency plan. I guess I've outlined a number of those options. You've acknowledged that you heard those as part of presentation and the testimony. We'll continue to look at those alternatives using Soyuz as well as Progress vehicles, and we're also hopeful of an expeditious conclusion that would tell us what occurred on Shuttle *Columbia* that would give us an opportunity to return to flight expeditiously.

All those factors are in play. Those are all part of that contingency plan. I think the specific reference in this case from the testimony you cite, was no way to get back with Shuttle immediately given the safety considerations that we will always ground the fleet under those circumstances.

I fully concur on your opening comments, too, as it pertains to charter revisions, to the extent they are necessary. As I pledged to Chairman Boehlert, we will make those changes in any way that Admiral Gehman feels he has to have in order to guarantee that independence.

I have no difficult whatsoever understanding his requirements for independence, and he has reiterated those, and I intend to comply exactly with that approach.

Chairman **MCCAIN.** Senator Fitzgerald.

Questioning an Aging System

Senator **FITZGERALD.** Thank you, Mr. Chairman.

Mr. O'Keefe, the day after the *Columbia* accident, I happened to be having a town hall meeting in Champaign, Illinois, and I asked—there were about two, maybe two-hundred-fifty, people in the room—I asked them whether they thought we should continue with manned exploration of space, and I explained to them that it could cost us billions of dollars and years to make ourselves able to continue going forward in space.

To my surprise, I'd say about four-fifths of the people in that room wanted us to go back and continue human exploration of space. And my state of Illinois has very little in the way of spending that it benefits from. We're not Florida or Texas. And I want the space program to continue.

And I wondered if you had a gut impression at this point—and I know it's early, but it seems to me we can go in one of two directions. We could spend billions of dollars and perhaps years trying to patch up and fix whatever may be wrong with the Shuttle program, but you're basically dealing with a 30-year-old design. My understanding is there are some 1.2 million checks that have to be done by hundreds of people before a single Shuttle flight can take off. It's extraordinarily complex.

My question is, Do we go forward and spend that time and that money reinforcing the Shuttle program, or would we be better off not diverting the resources to reinforcing this 30-year-old Shuttle program, and, instead, try and proceed with a new vehicle and focus all our effort on that?

Mr. **O'KEEFE.** Well, thank you, Senator. The factors, I think, that lead to the complexity of the Shuttle and the amount of checking that goes on there certainly is driven by the technology, no doubt about that, the number of moving parts on that asset. But I would submit that any asset we have that we would use, for the purpose of a Reusable Launch Vehicle capability to launch, would also require an awful lot of checks, as well, because of the absolute dedication, the unwavering commitment to safety, that we always pursue.

Every time we launch a Shuttle flight, no matter what that asset would be, it would require, I think, a review of all the systems checks. And the ethos that we have within the agency and all that are part of the community is that if there's a single thing that is wrong or that appears to be wrong in the judgment of any individual, there is a process set up to stop the launch.

Two weeks in advance, there's a Flight Readiness Review that runs to ground every issue involved in that. If there's any residual issues all the way up to the moment of launch, we don't do that. I don't envision that changing. Even if we had a system today that was brand new, I think that same ethos would have to dominate, because we really are committed to that objective to minimize the risk. We'll never drive the risk out of it completely. And so I think that same approach would be employed no matter what assets or capabilities.

Having said all that, if the investigation leads us to conclude that there is anything structurally deficient about the continued safe operations of the Shuttle system, we positively will take that as a very strong element of the investigation findings and make judgments accordingly that may lead us in the kinds of directions you're talking about.

In the interim, again, our approach is, as I discussed with Congressman Rohrabacher, we tear down this system about every eight to ten flights, essentially rebuild it as new, and it goes through that 18- to 24-month Orbiter Major Modification Program. And so every time that asset goes up there, it is as safe as we know how to make it.

We'll never drive the risk out entirely, but we're trying to manage it down to the lowest possible level and assure that anything that appears even vaguely awry is beaten to parade rest before we let the flight take off, and during orbit, as well.

Chairman **BOEHLERT.** The gentleman's time has expired.

Mr. Calvert.

Representative **CALVERT.** Thank you, Mr. Chairman.

Thank you, Mr. O'Keefe, for attending today. And certainly my sympathies to the family and to the NASA family that's certainly still grieving over this loss.

I think all of us here today share one thing, and that's that we desire an independent assessment, unbiased and with the highest integrity, to ensure that future astronauts, NASA, this Congress, and the country have confidence in its ultimate result. Certainly you're off to a good start, and I certainly appreciate that, and I know that we do and the country does. But as Chairman Boehlert has indicated, it may be necessary that changes be made to make sure we maintain that confidence. And I'm thankful that you're open-minded to that.

It's reported that we have a certain amount of money appropriated, I believe about $50 million, for NASA to complete this investigation. Is that funding adequate to pursue, in your mind, to the levels that we're discussing?

Mr. **O'KEEFE.** I don't know, sir. As I understand it, that's part of the current appropriations conference deliberations. I've read the same press accounts you have. I have no other knowledge of what you and your colleagues may have in mind for that Omnibus Appropriations bill provision, and so I can't make an assessment of that. And I don't know what the cost of this will be, other than to say that whatever it costs, that's what we ought to spend in order to be sure that we reach the answers to what caused this accident.

Representative **CALVERT.** Obviously, NASA is not the only agency that's going to be involved in this investigation. Are you receiving cooperation from other agencies, full cooperation?

Mr. **O'KEEFE.** Yes, sir. It's overwhelming. There is no hesitancy, there is no confusion of how that process works. I've just been amazed to see how forward-leaning 20 different Federal agencies, state and local law enforcement officials from Texas and Louisiana, have been in helping us work through what is a real nightmarish circumstance in a way that's professional, aboveboard, and fully cooperative. No hesitation on that point at all.

Representative **CALVERT.** And that also would apply to the contractors that are involved in this program?

Mr. **O'KEEFE.** Yes, sir, absolutely.

Representative **CALVERT.** I know I've read the press quotes. You mentioned, just as of yesterday, that you had no favorite theories of what occurred, and I understand that. However, as we move forward in this Congress, I guess that what Mr. Rohrabacher and others have indicated, do you believe, because of the age of the Shuttle, there is any systemic problem that may be there? And what's our alternatives if, in fact, that's the case?

Mr. **O'KEEFE.** Again, none that I'm aware of. And, again, we go through an exhaustive process to assure that that the safety-of-flight operation is adhered each and every time. This is not a one-shot deal. It's every—every time it comes back, the orbiters return, we do a careful inspection, we go through a very exhaustive review of everything, and we do not roll it out immediately. There's an orbiter processing facility effort that goes on for the better part of three months as we move it through an exhaustive examination. And then when it gets out to the launch pad, typically it's there for the better part of 30 days in order to make sure that every single thing checks out.

So if there's something systemically wrong, we will be guided by the Gehman board's view of that and we'll correct it. But based on our assessment right now and everything we've done, it sure doesn't look like a systemic failure. But if it is, we positively will correct that before we launch ever again.

Representative **CALVERT.** Thank you.

Mr. **O'KEEFE.** Thank you, sir.

Representative **CALVERT.** Thank you, Mr. Chairman.

Chairman **MCCAIN.** Senator Dorgan.

Suggesting a Presidential Commission

Senator **DORGAN.** Mr. O'Keefe, thank you for being here today. I think most of us feel that a nation that doesn't explore is a nation that's standing still, and this space program must continue exploring the frontiers of space.

I want to ask you a question, and I don't want you to think the origin of my question poses any distrust for you or the men and women of NASA. I have great admiration for your leadership and also for the men and women of NASA. But as we attempt to find out what happened with this tragedy, it seems to me that in almost any circumstance of this type, an agency can't very effectively investigate itself. I feel there ought to be a Presidential Commission empaneled. I would ask the question, Have you had a chance to visit with President Bush about the prospect of that? And can it be done enveloping reconfiguring the kind of commission that you have now created?

Mr. **O'KEEFE.** Yes, sir. Oh, yes, indeed, we have visited on the question, to the President as well as the Vice President and all the senior staff on the issue. And I guess the approach that—history is a guide in these cases.

In the *Challenger* accident, it was five days after the accident that President Reagan announced the intent to appoint a commission. It was the better part of 10 days to two weeks before they assembled. It was probably the better end of three to four weeks before they were fully prepared to engage and really start taking testimony and doing the things that were necessary. And they still, nonetheless, produced a set of findings and recommendations by June of 1986. So roughly six months after the accident they were able to reach some conclusions.

In this circumstance, given the development of this contingency plan that we've put together as a lesson learned from *Challenger,* and there was an awful lot that we learned out of that event, that really informed us about how we ought to go ahead and look at ourselves and how we do business. And what it called for as part of that contingency plan was to identify, by positions, the kinds of people that ought to be activated, who are non-NASA individuals and experts, and mobilize them right away.

And so as a consequence, what we defaulted in favor of in this case was speed. We had an opportunity then to have all the members except one, who was a NASA center director of a non-space-flight center, who has no involvement with space flight at all, who was appointed to that particular board. Everybody else is removed from it, and we're moving ahead in that regard as independent as we can possibly make that.

Senator **DORGAN.** Can I make the point that I think you did exactly the right thing, because you don't want time to elapse. You took action and did the right thing. I'm asking, I guess, as we go along, whether a presidential commission can now envelope, reconfigure the commission that you have started.

I really do think that a year from now, three, five years from now, the question people will ask is, Could NASA really have investigated itself? Again, I don't say that with any distrust at all. I think you've got a great organization. But I really do hope, as we go along here, we're finding a way to perhaps have a Presidential Commission. We don't want to duplicate different investigations, but I think this could be done in the right way and will resolve these questions of independence.

Mr. **O'KEEFE.** Yes, sir.

Senator **DORGAN.** So let me wish you well, and please extend, on behalf of all of us in the Congress, our thoughts and prayers to the men and women of NASA.

Mr. **O'KEEFE.** Thank you, Senator. We're committed to

exactly the same objective. We want to find the answers, and we want it to be credible. I mean, there's no question about that at all. So whatever it's going to take in order to do that, that's what we are committed to doing.

And the process, again, is not investigating ourselves. This is an independent group of folks who have no, baggage to carry as it pertains to, NASA biases. Admiral Gehman came from a distinguished naval career that had no involvement whatsoever with NASA, and yet, at the same time, I think he's had a lot of experience, as all the other members did, of better than 50 different investigations into accident situations.

So this is not a group of NASA investigating itself. This is going to be an independent group that's going to reach some conclusions, and we want to make sure that's as credible as we can possibly make it, because that's going to turn on—I think the trust and confidence of the American people depend upon that. Your point is exactly right. I associate myself with that sentiment, as well.

Chairman **BOEHLERT.** Mr. Lampson.

Representative **LAMPSON.** I want to thank you, Mr. O'Keefe, for coming to Capitol Hill to testify today. As the member of Congress who represents the Johnson Space Center, I would also like to thank you and your NASA team for the support and encouragement that you've provided to the space center community in Houston during this very difficult time.

I'm somewhat of a reluctant participant in this hearing. Today is the 11th day since the tragic loss of Space Shuttle *Columbia*. There's so much that we do not yet know and perhaps some things that we may never know.

It's my understanding that there were no Congressional hearings on the *Challenger* investigation in 1986 until after the Rogers

Commission completed their report four months later. And while I know we're operating under different circumstances, with three astronauts orbiting the Earth in the International Space Station, I do question the merits of having this hearing so soon after the *Columbia* Shuttle accident.

I believe Congress needs to allow the investigation to move forward and to let the accident investigation board members do their work. Hopefully we will complement your efforts and not impede the process.

That being said, I firmly believe that the Administration needs to move forward with a truly independent investigation similar to what President Reagan appointed in 1986 after the *Challenger* accident.

I think NASA made a good first step by revising the board's charter last week, but I still believe, as my colleagues have stated, that NASA's external investigation team is too closely tied to the agency.

As NASA Administrator, the board's charter allows you to appoint the team members, to staff the board with NASA employees, and to receive the final report. In order for this review to have credibility, I believe it needs to have team members who are truly independent and who report to the White House and Congress.

Also, seeing all the cameras and the media presence in this hearing room today begs the question, Where was all this attention to our human space flight programs before February 1st? While I applaud the renewed interest, I regret that it takes the loss of seven fine astronauts for our space program to make the front page of the newspaper or the top story on the evening news.

And while it may seem routine, the work that is being done by

NASA in outer space is far from routine. We're doing so many great things in space that benefit us right here on Earth. My hope is that somehow this terrible tragedy will spur the Administration to develop an interest in a real, truly robust space program.

And I'd like to call for a new space race for the 21st century. This space race is not against the old Cold War enemy or an emerging power in the East, but rather our new space race needs to be against ourselves for our own future.

ISS Contingency Planning

And let me ask two things, Mr. O'Keefe. First, a copy of the contingency plan for the International Space Station that you referred to a few minutes ago, could you possibly get that to us within the next week or so? We would appreciate it.

[The information follows:]

Copies of the following documents have been provided to the Committee:

85090ww.eps

And then let me ask, in 1999, when problems with the experimental X–33 Reusable Launch Vehicle demonstrator made it clear the Space Shuttle would have to be relied on for many more years, perhaps until 2020, the Clinton Administration's OMB sensibly increased the Shuttle upgrades budget significantly. However, in 2001, the Bush Administration's OMB, of which you were deputy director, simultaneously cancelled X–33 program and cut the Space Shuttle safety upgrades budget. How can that possibly have made sense, and can you tell us why you did that?

Mr. **O'KEEFE.** Again, I'd have to go back and take a look at when NASA cancelled the X–33 program and exactly what was leading to that particular case. But if I can get slide 16, please? The history over the course of time, as I understand it, was a span that you'll see on this particular slide that was for Shuttle funding over the course of that time. The increase that you see occurred, again, as part of the fiscal year '03 budget proposal that we made, and '04, that was just submitted to the Congress last Monday.

So my reading of the data and the information is that there's an awful lot that contributed to this particular change in funding profile over this span of time, but it was primarily driven by a concurrent, I think, focus on safety improvements and kind of concentrating on all of the factors that would lead to safe-flight operations, and, concurrently, efficiencies that drove down the cost of guaranteeing those particular safe-flight operations through the '90's.

And the most significant increase that's occurred is part of the fiscal year '03 budget amendment the President submitted last November, and the fiscal year '04 budget was submitted last Monday. So those are the primary increases that I've been able to examine, but I'd certainly be prepared to submit all that for the record for your consideration, sir.

Representative **LAMPSON.** Thank you.

Chairman **MCCAIN.** Senator Allen.

Mr. **O'KEEFE.** One other comment, if I could, Senator, is just to reiterate again that the Gehman Commission will report to all of us. He's going to report to the President, to Congress, to all the American people as soon as they reach findings. I have no intention whatsoever of putting any value added to their findings. As soon as the ink is dry, it will be released by Hal Gehman. There is no other approach that I can think of that would be a more appropriate way to handle this so we can move on with finding what the solution is to the problem, get the answers to it, and make the corrections necessary to get back to flying safety.

Representative **LAMPSON.** Thank you.

Chairman **MCCAIN.** Senator Allen.

Role of Automation and Robotics

Senator **ALLEN.** Thank you, Mr. Chairman. Thank you, Mr. O'Keefe, for being here.

I want to associate myself with some of the thoughts and philosophy stated in the beginning by our chairman, Senator McCain. And I want to focus on the long-term goals of NASA, broader goals.

If anything good can come out of this tragedy, I think it would be the reinvigorated focus on the mission, primary mission, of NASA, which ought to be scientific research that has benefit for people here on Earth. And I think such sensible strategic planning would be a salutary goal and part of the legacy of the tragic loss of these brave men and women. And I know that of paramount concern to you and all the people in NASA is safety, safety for humans primarily.

Previously, before this tragedy, I know you're on record as supporting refurbished or upgraded Shuttles so they can remain operational for the next 10 to 20 years. I think, in examining the broader goals of NASA, it would be helpful if we'd have some consideration of what is going to be the next orbiter. There are so many questions that we have to determine, and this is just the beginning of this examination. Once we get into our committees in the House and Senate, we'll get in greater detail.

But my question is specific on automation and robotics, and how can robotics and automation and advances in technology, how can that make it safer? It is less costly, but it's also safer for human life. And so is NASA considering an entirely new space plane orbiter or downsizing the manned space flight? Depending on which option is chosen, how will that shape our efforts, our efforts also as the $30 billion, of course, that we've already invested in this space station, the International Space Station, as an investment? But where are we in embracing some of these advancements in automation and robotics? And in the strategic planning, will it effect the continued dangerously underfunding of aeronautics, which I think have tangible benefits to us militarily as well as in the commercial markets?

So I'd like your thoughts on these key paths that we need to go down and decide which ones we're going to go down in the future.

Mr. **O'KEEFE.** Thank you, Senator. It is, in my judgment, not an issue of either/or, robotics or human space flight. It's how do you do it compatibly? How do you find the appropriate role for robotic capabilities that set, in advance, the kind of knowledge base that you need in order to then support, when necessary, and in circumstances where human intervention and human involvement then becomes very critical.

Again, the Hubble Telescope is the classic example. It's a marvelous piece of machinery that didn't work, and the only way it could be adjusted was to have human involvement in order to make those adjustments on each of the respective servicing missions that have gone on. And now it is rewriting the astronomy books. It is a classic example of how that compatibility between robotics and the use of human space flight intervention, when necessary, can advance the knowledge base dramatically.

But we have to really focus on the risk management side of this and assure that we always use those robotic capabilities, I think, as you've suggested, as a way to fully beat down any of the manageable risk that we see before involving a human space flight capability for that reason, as well as being careful about when you utilize the human involvement dimension to this. That's part of the reason, and a lot of the reason, why the Mars program that we're pursuing for the Mars landers that are planned for later this year and arriving in January of '04 is to advance that knowledge base, understanding fully what's going on in order to then fully support what could be, down the road, a human—a mission that could support that case, if deemed appropriate, necessary, and supported by the research and the science opportunities that could be yielded.

So the strategy you've talked about and the approach that you're alluding to is precisely the direction we're trying to develop now, and have been for some time, as a means to complement those capabilities and always use the robotic capacity up front as the means to inform those judgments.

Chairman **BOEHLERT.** The gentleman's time has expired.

Mr. Lucas.

Representative **LUCAS.** Thank you, Mr. Chairman.

Mr. Administrator, down at the Smithsonian, they have a piece of your old equipment hanging for all the world to see, the X–15 from the 1960's, which is a symbol of a debate and a decision by the generation ahead of you and I that, in the spirit of satisfying the common need of the United States Congress and the American people for immediate gratification, it was better to strap men and women and equipment on ballistic missiles than it was to focus on creating space planes.

Your comments today—you point out about the potential future for an Orbital Space Plane and the Reusable Launch Vehicles— with reasonable budget and reasonable focus, how far down the road are we talking about before we have functioning replacement systems like that?

Mr. **O'KEEFE.** Well, the budget before the Congress as part of the amended fiscal year '03 proposal the President made last November, would contemplate a technology demonstrator of the Orbital Space Plane as early as fiscal year '06, flight testing and so forth to occur as soon as next summer that would lead up to that technology demonstrator. Then, from there to developing as we've now completed the essential baseline requirements, if you will, look for competing approaches—not a technology demonstrator, but an operational vehicle—that would accomplish the objectives of both rescue and return capacity as well as transfer to the International Space Station. It would be online, we would hope, as early as the end of this decade, and we're kind of moving in that direction to try to establish that.

This would be a complementary capability to the Space Shuttle and use the Space Shuttle primarily as a cargo capacity, heavy-lift ability, rather than trying to make a vehicle that's all things to all requirements. This would be a crew transfer capability that would be maneuverable, flexible, and responsive to those kinds of circumstances where needed most.

Representative **LUCAS.** Booster, slash, plane, or a two-stage plane, Administrator?

Mr. **O'KEEFE.** It is initially planned as a capability mounted atop an Expendable Launch Vehicle. And that technology demonstrator will be that initial capability that we will utilize at that time.

Representative **LUCAS.** Along that line, since it's obvious that, with that amount of effort required and the need, as you've pointed out so succinctly, to keep the workhorse, the old Shuttle, up and going, could you address for a moment some of the discussion we've had on the committee for some time about the effect on the reduction in the number of people who—full-time employees who support the Shuttle over the last decade—literally, what, one-third less people still making, if not the same number, but even a greater number of safety checks?

Mr. **O'KEEFE.** Absolutely. I think the history appears to suggest—and, again, we'll be guided a lot by the review that the investigation board will go through in terms of looking at the systemic causes of what may have been there. So their charter is very broad, and their scope is rather extensive. But it would appear as though that the—exactly as you've suggested, the history is that while cost reductions and efficiencies were gained over the course of that period, as previously described on a slide, there were also improvements in the safety margins as well as the reduction of incidents prior to launch, on-orbit incidents, you name it, there were—all the trends were moving in a direction that proved or demonstrated greater efficiency in addition to slide 18, if you will, that would prove the capabilities, I think, that have significantly improved over the span, both decreasing incidents and increasing efficiencies.

But, again, all that is, is based on the data and the information we see over this particular trend line. We're going to be guided by what the systemic causes are that the investigation board may come back and look at for this information and say that may or may not have been a contributing factor to it. And we'll be guided by their view.

Representative **LUCAS.** Thank you, Administrator.

Mr. **O'KEEFE.** Thank you, sir.

Chairman **MCCAIN.** Senator Boxer.

Senator **BOXER.** Thank you very much.

Mr. O'Keefe, I want to join my colleagues in sending my condolences to the families and also my feelings of condolence, as well, to NASA. In California, we're the birthplace of the Shuttle program. We hold a very special place in our heart for the heroes who conduct these flights. And it's in this spirit that I ask my questions.

Crew Escape Systems

In the year 2000, your safety panel made a very clear recommendation. I ask unanimous consent that I place this page in the record. I trust, without objection, that will be done.

Senator **BOXER.** This is a quote, "The Presidential Commission on the Shuttle *Challenger* Accident addressed crew escape in their report and recommended that NASA make all efforts to provide a crew escape system. NASA responded by initiating crew escape studies." This is in this safety panel. Then it says, "Over the lifetime of the Space Shuttle, the reliable post-launch crew escape system will provide the largest potential improvement in crew safety. NASA has completed or has underway a number of studies that also suggest such a system is feasible." And then they say, "The time is past due for the implementation of a more capable crew escape system."

Now, Mr. O'Keefe, after that report was filed, members of the safety panel were fired. And I ask unanimous consent to put in the record the New York Times story entitled *NASA Dismissed Advisors Who Warned About Safety.*

Mr. Chairman, will you put that in the record for me? Mr. Chairman? Mr. Chairman?

Chairman **BOEHLERT.** Without objection.

Senator **BOXER.** Thank you.

Senator **BOXER.** And after that report and after the people were fired, four board members were fired, two consultants were fired, one board member quit because he was upset at the firings. That left you two people. You changed the charter of the panel.

And I ask unanimous consent that the new charter and the old charter be placed in the record.

Chairman **BOEHLERT.** Without objection.

Senator **BOXER.** And, in essence, without going through the bureaucratic talk in here, the new charter, Mr. O'Keefe, gives you much more power—the NASA Administrator, not you personally; in this case, you personally—more power to essentially veto who they choose as chair of the panel.

So I put all these pieces together, Mr. Chairman, and I have concern. I see a report that clearly doesn't mince words here that time is past due for the implementation of a more capable crew escape system. I see members being fired. I then see a new charter where now there's less independence of the safety panel.

I want to know how you feel about this array of facts. First of all, do you agree that the time is past due for the implementation of a more capable crew escape system? And if you do, why haven't we seen more done about it? Number two, why do you think those folks were fired? And, number three, would agree, in light of your, I believe, very sincere comments that safety is a priority, that you would go back to the old charter where the panel could choose its own leader and not have the NASA administrator veto it?

Mr. **O'KEEFE.** Well, thank you, Senator.

On the first issue, as it pertains to crew escape, again there were a series of very important recommendations that came from the Rogers Commission or outgrowths of the post-*Challenger* experience—that changed operational procedures as it pertained to crew escape and capabilities that were recommended therein. And prior to launch, there is a complete safety regime that's in place that didn't exist prior to the *Challenger,* because of their recommendations. It's a very significant change.

Having said that, my understanding is that the analysis that went on a couple or three years ago following that particular set of reports of the options all led to a series of technical modifications to the Shuttle which have increased its weight dramatically, its operations, its maneuverability, and so, therefore, were deemed to be a marginal improvement in safety that could be attained, if at all, and yet dramatically increased weight, which would have compromised the safety of on-orbit capabilities.

Senator **BOXER.** So you didn't agree with this recommendation of the——

Chairman **MCCAIN.** And the gentlewoman's time is expired.

Mr. **O'KEEFE.** No, I——

Senator **BOXER.** Well, Mr. Chairman, I'm just trying to see——
——

Chairman **MCCAIN.** No, I'm sorry, the gentlewoman's time has expired.

Senator **BOXER.** I know that you're sorry.

Chairman **MCCAIN.** Go ahead. We'll recognize the next——

Senator **BOXER.** I know that you're sorry. Thank you.

Mr. **O'KEEFE.** I'm sorry, Senator.

No, it is—my agreement, notwithstanding or not, I, again, am not fully aware of all of the parameters of it. I'm advised that's what led the folks to conclude two or three years ago.

Having said that, we are going to look at anything that the investigative board comes back with and says, "These are the changes that must be made in order to guarantee safe flight operations." If it contains that particular set of questions, which, by the way, were primarily pertaining to, as I understand it, ascent requirements, not descent capabilities, that, in turn, those kinds of requirements be factored in and that we make the changes appropriate to do so.

To your second point as it pertains to the safety panel board composition, its charter, and so forth, that occurred prior to my tenure. I don't know exactly what the circumstances were, short of the press accounts and the folklore or legend that may have gone into who did what to who when. Nonetheless, I do understand that, in '97, based on a report from the Inspector General at that time, offered as how a cadre of panel members with long-term experience and in-depth NASA knowledge is important. But to be most effective, this group must be routinely infused with the fresh perspective of new, diverse members. So, as a consequence, the Inspector General's position, as I understand it, was acted upon by my predecessor.

Suggestions were made as to the charter to limit the duration of the tenure to two terms, I believe, of six years each. We'll certainly go back and re-examine that. If it's the desire on the part of the panel members to look at a different tenure period of time that they think enhances their wisdom and understanding of the safety issues, I am all ears on that.

The prior chairman introduced himself to me within 30 days of my arrival at NASA as the outgoing chairman. So I don't know how they arrived at who was going to become the chairman and who would be the next chairperson, but the current chair is the individual that was anointed and appointed, I guess by me, but with the concurrence of the board prior to that time. I made no objection to it. And the only individual who is new to the board is one individual who was added to it during the course of my tenure. No one else has been released.

So I've really been trying to look at what the composition of the panel is, and assure its advisory status, that's the strongest we can possibly make it, and changes made prior to that we'll certainly go back and revisit to assure that if they have different views that would enhance or strengthen their position, that's what we want to hear. We want to make sure that safety of operation is adhered to at all times.

Chairman BOEHLERT. Thank you very much.

Mr. Udall.

Chairman MCCAIN. Could I just say, I want to apologize to all members for enforcing the time limits. We do have such a large number of questioners, and our members have been very patient, and I appreciate that.

Chairman BOEHLERT. Mr. Udall.

Representative UDALL. Thank you, Mr. Chairman.

I, too, want to thank Mr. O'Keefe for taking his time to join us today. And I found your testimony insightful, enlightening, and, in fact, quite moving, and I want to thank you for your leadership.

Mr. **O'KEEFE.** Thank you.

Representative **UDALL.** I know you're beginning to think you're in an echo chamber, but I did also want to associate myself with the remarks of our Chairman on the House side and the Ranking Member and others, who have urged you to create as independent a commission as possible and that we'll all be well served when those results are announced.

Mr. **O'KEEFE.** Yes, sir.

Representative **UDALL.** In my experience in my previous career as an outdoor educator and someone who was very involved in the climbing and mountaineering communities, we found that when we had accidents, that independent entities that had no fiduciary relationship or other relationship with those involved could make quite accurate and objective determinations of what occurred. So I want to lend my voice to those of others here.

Mr. **O'KEEFE.** Yes, sir.

Representative **UDALL.** I did also want to acknowledge the tremendous sacrifice and the bravery of our astronauts and send my condolences to the family members and friends of the brave astronauts. We in Colorado have a proud history of involvement with NASA. In fact, Kalpana Chawla was one of the members of the crew, and she was a graduate of the University of Colorado, so we feel that loss very deeply in Colorado.

Mr. Chairman, if I might, I'd like to include in the record an article from the New York Times on Monday, February 10th, that talks about all the tremendous benefits that have been generated by the space program. I know there are some——

Chairman **BOEHLERT.** Without objection, so ordered.

Representative **UDALL.** Thank you.

Replacing the Space Shuttle Orbiter

Representative **UDALL.** There have been debates and discussions and comments that the astronauts were involved in minor science projects while they were orbiting the Earth. And I think if you look into the record, in fact, what's resulted from our space program is truly remarkable, and day in and day out we see the results of those advancements here on Earth.

If I could, I'd like to focus a little bit on the Space Shuttle orbiter and whether we ought to replace it. Have you gotten to the point where you have an opinion in that regard about the replacement of the Space Shuttle orbiter?

Mr. **O'KEEFE.** Yes, sir. The Integrated Space Transportation Plan we're currently working with was devised over the course of last year and culminating in the November 13th, 2002, amendment that the President submitted to the 2003 budget that the Congress is still deliberating on at this time. It's reinforced in the 2004 budget submission the President made last Monday, which is to look at all the elements of how these particular systems support each other.

I think, for a long time, all the trends seemed to suggest that every one of these were looked at as individual, standalone programs. But there's a great interrelationship between them. And the requirement for Space Shuttle capabilities, both in terms of crew transfer, which is how we typically have rotated the crews aboard the International Space Station, as well as the launch of cargo assets—in other words, all of the new pieces that are being installed on International Space Station to build out that laboratory that can't be duplicated here on Earth—is a capability we've really got to look at in relationship to each other and to consider a crew transfer and rescue return capacity that can be introduced more aggressively than we presently have.

So the combination of both Shuttle and how we maintain its cargo lift capacity for capabilities to continue to not only support, but finish building, the International Space Station, the capability to transfer crew in order to rotate the expedition crews that we've seen now in our—here we are in our third year of permanent presence onboard that system—as well as the Orbital Space Plane that would provide that capability, all three of those dimensions and the Next-Generation Launch Technologies to ultimately replace the cargo capacity is our focus in that amendment, as well as in the present budget before the Congress right now.

Representative **UDALL.** Mr. Chairman, I don't know where my time is, but what is the status of the orbiter——

Chairman **MCCAIN.** Your time has expired.

Senator Wyden.

Senator **WYDEN.** Thank you, Mr. Chairman.

Administrator O'Keefe, when I chaired your confirmation hearings, I found you to be honest and candid, and we're going to need an awful lot of that in the days ahead, and we appreciate your being here.

NASA Workforce Legislation

My first question deals with the huge brain-drain situation at NASA. It seems to me that you all are hemorrhaging talent in key areas, like electrical engineering. And I think this has implications both for the short-term and the long-term.

The February 1st date, for example, on that date, you all were being pushed to, in effect, use more outside contractors and fewer people within the agency, and so some, of course, are saying that when we have a chance to study this, it's going to back "the people."

So I'd like you to comment on the brain-drain problem, both from the short-term and the long-term, and what's being done to address it.

Mr. **O'KEEFE.** Thank you, Senator.

Indeed, that is a concern that, as we've discussed previously, as well as we've talked about in various hearings, over the course of the last dozen years or so, we've seen a very clear trend in the direction of an aging workforce that are capable, very strong professionals, but it is, nonetheless, a very mature workforce. We've got three times as many scientists and engineers that are over 60 as we have under 30. And so the consequence of that set of decisions made in years gone by of bringing in additional talent at gradations, there's no way to instantly grow longevity as well as experience base.

What we submitted last June to the Congress was a series of legislative initiatives specifically focused on strategic management of human capital, as has been advised by the General Accounting Office. Dave Walker, as the Comptroller General, has consistently talked about this. So we forwarded this series of legislative provisions. They have been sent to the Congress, they're in the appropriate committees of jurisdiction, and are under consideration to try to deal with what those tools would be that we could use for the purpose of not only retaining for the near-term period the kinds of capabilities and talent we have today, but also recruiting talent with some experience base with a variety of walks and backgrounds, as well as bringing in new graduate students and doctoral students who would replace that roughly 60 percent of the workforce that is of scientific and technical background. You're exactly right, it's a concern, and we want to act on it.

Senator **WYDEN.** I want to ask——

Mr. **O'KEEFE.** We look for to the Congress' early enactment of all those provisions to move us along that way.

Senator **WYDEN.** I want to ask one other quick question. I think when we get to the bottom of this, I think we're going to see that we've got to address this issue, and I just pray that this tragic loss hasn't been due to some human error.

Manned vs. Unmanned Spacecraft

The second question I had deals with manned versus unmanned space flight. I think that manned flights represent the aspirations and hopes of so many Americans, but I will tell you, I personally believe we're going to need to do more in the unmanned area. I think it is going to be an imperative in the days ahead. And I'd like your judgment as to how to make that call.

For example, I'm attracted to the argument that when you're talking about the space station a few hundred miles, you know, up, that wouldn't be as high a priority as really looking to distant worlds. But I'd be curious how you'd go about tackling this question and making the tough calls with respect to manned versus unmanned space flight. I want to see the manned expeditions go forward, but I do think we're going to have to have a bigger role for unmanned expeditions in the days ahead, and I'd like to hear you tell us how you'd go about making those calls.

Mr. **O'KEEFE.** Sure, thank you, Senator. I think you've hit the nail right on the head.

The strategy we've tried to employ here, again, is not an either/or, but very much a combination of how do you best employ the robotic capabilities that we have to advance our knowledge base and understand what the challenges will be in order to assure the greatest probability of safety of flight operations when and if called upon to engage humans in that science and research set of objectives.

So the approach that we've devised, for example, in the case of the Mars landers that are planned, and explorers that are planned, for later this year, due to arrive there in early '04, is to continue to build that knowledge base understanding the challenges and difficulties we will work with.

And the inhibitors on exploration much beyond where we are today typically are human related, to be sure, but it's partly technology related. The first one is that our limitations on capacity for propulsion, speed, to get anywhere is currently restricted by the same laws of physics we've been living with for 40 years. And so as a result, until we develop a new space propulsion capacity to dramatically reduce the time as well as the capacity to get anywhere, we're going to be really restricted, in terms of the capabilities we have in that regard.

The second is how to assure that humans survive the experience. And as it stands now, the exposure that we see and that we're learning on International Space Station as a consequence of long duration spaceflight are the debilitating effects on human beings of space travel and space exploration. We're looking to conquer those. Part of the budget proposal you have before you as part of the '04 submission that the President just made is an intensive effort to look at human factors. And only then, after we've conquered those kinds of challenges of degradation, of muscle mass, bone mass, radiation effects, all those things, should we venture much beyond where we have the capacity to do today, which is a very important pursuit of science and research aboard station and other objectives.

So the whole strategy here is to lay this out in a way that informs the knowledge base by robotic capabilities, follow along to the extent necessary and when human intervention gives us the opportunity to expand that knowledge base, and make sure they can only do it when there's a safety-of-flight capability that we can assure.

Senator **WYDEN.** Thank you, Mr. Chairman.

Mr. **O'KEEFE.** Thank you, Senator. I appreciate it very much.

Chairman **BOEHLERT.** Mr. Weldon.

Representative **WELDON.** Thank you, Mr. Chairman.

Administrator O'Keefe, thank you for coming. And I have the highest confidence in your leadership, as I do in Admiral Gehman's leadership, who did an outstanding job in investigating the USS Cole.

Thermal Tile Adhesive

I have a very specific series of questions that you may not be able to answer here, but I would like a thorough response for the record, relative to one aspect of the operations of the Shuttle, and it deals with the tiles.

The tiles are glued to the Shuttle by a special adhesive. That adhesive has, as it's primary component, urea. The urea that's produced is produced around the world, and much of it's for agriculture and industrial purposes. But the specific urea that NASA has used for the glue for the tiles was produced by one plant, and that one plant was in Fort Saskatchewan, Alberta, Canada. And the reason why that plant was selected was because none of the U.S. manufacturers were able to meet the very stringent requirements that NASA had established for the urea, for the glue for the tiles.

About five years ago, that plant was acquired by another Canadian firm that does business in Cuba. And because of that, they were concerned about the implications of Helms-Burton legislation, and so they no longer supplied NASA the urea for the glue for the tiles.

The U.S. manufacturer of the adhesive that used that specific urea was very concerned at the time about finding a new source of urea that would meet the very specific, tough requirements that NASA had for the glue to hold the tiles on. And I would say there are millions of tons of urea consumed in the U.S. every year. But only a very, very small portion of it would be used specifically by NASA for the glue for the tiles. And, as I said before, up until that takeover five years ago, it was from one plant in Canada that had a separate mechanism for producing that urea that U.S. manufacturers did not, or perhaps could not, achieve the same quality standards that NASA required.

So what my concern is, whether or not we found an equally reliable supplier of urea. And, for the record, I'd like you to give us that information relative to the specifics of NASA specifications.

Thank you.

Mr. **O'KEEFE.** Yes, sir. No, I don't know. I really am not aware of the nuances there, but I positively will provide that for the record.

Representative **WELDON.** Thank you.

Mr. **O'KEEFE.** Thank you, sir.

Representative **WELDON.** Thank you, Mr. Chairman.

Senator **BROWNBACK.** Senator Snowe.

Senator **SNOWE.** Thank you, Mr. Chairman. And welcome, Mr. O'Keefe. I know this a very trying time for you and the NASA family and most certainly the families of the astronauts. And it just reminds us how fortunate we are as a nation to have been blessed with men and women like these astronauts who are willing to take risks for this country.

Debris Assessment and Need for Imagery

I'm trying to get at the picture of how NASA approaches certain decisions—what is minimized, what is discounted. We know that for 12 days, from the time that you all learned of the debris that hit the Shuttle and then the Shuttle was scheduled to land, no action was taken other than doing some computer model simulations to predict damage and to rely on past experiences where Shuttles had returned safely, even though there had been several Stanford studies in 1990 and 1994 that had already warned of some potential damage that a single piece of debris could have had on the tiles.

Could you tell me as to why no request was made for military telescope imaging? We know that a camera was not working at the time of orbit that really could have shown the damage that was done on the underside of the Shuttle. Why wasn't that requested at some point in time during the flight to do a greater examination of this type of damage, rather than relying on computer modeling when you really didn't know what had happened, rather than doing the modeling on something that you knew had happened?

Mr. **O'KEEFE.** Thank you, Senator.

The investigative process, and certainly the Gehman Board, if they come to find we should have done something else, positively we'll be, you know, guided by that particular finding. Nonetheless, the approach that was taken here is, this is a piece of foam material that was about a foot and a half by six inches of which there have been incidents like this before. And, as I mentioned earlier, there are cases where after the flight, there's a full examination of every square inch, every single element of the orbiter when it comes back, to see what the damage effect was. It was determined, in previous cases of comparable circumstance, not to have been a safety-of-flight consideration.

Again, the circumstances here were, it came off of the external tank as the entire Shuttle orbiter system was traveling at 3600 miles an hour. The piece came off, dropped roughly 40 feet at a rate of something like 50 miles an hour, so it's the functional equivalent, as one astronaut described to me, of a Styrofoam cooler blowing off of a pickup truck ahead of you on a highway. And every incident we'd seen before that, every model we ran, every analysis that had been done on every prior case demonstrated no significant damage in that circumstance.

Of the 4,000 sensors aboard the Shuttle orbiter, none of them indicated any anomalies during that 16-day flight. And given the wide variation of heat of several hundred degrees that was experienced 16 times a day, if there was any penetration, any damage that could have been evident, the assumption was those sensors would have picked it up.

Nonetheless, if the Gehman Board finds that we really erred by not examining this in yet another direction, based on all the historical evidence, we positively will run that finding to ground and make corrective actions as necessary.

Senator **SNOWE.** But wasn't this piece of debris the largest documented piece ever to hit the Shuttle?

Mr. **O'KEEFE.** Not to my knowledge, but I will correct that for the record if that proves to be in error. I don't know whether that's true or not, but I certainly will provide that for the record.

Senator **SNOWE.** I guess——

Senator **BROWNBACK.** The time of the senator is up. I'm sorry.

Senator **SNOWE.** Thank you.

Chairman **BOEHLERT.** Mr. Wu.

Representative Wu. Thank you for being with us during a very difficult time, Mr. O'Keefe.

During my colleagues' questions, I took the liberty of drawing up a little diagram to illustrate my inquiry to you. It's not a PowerPoint presentation; it's just felt tip pen on a piece of paper. Across the bottom here, cuts in your budget. And going up, risk. And the red line is the typical hockey puck kind of curve that some of us in high tech like to see in financial returns, but we don't like to see in this kind of context.

And earlier, I heard you say that you are pounding out as much of the risk as possible before each and every Shuttle launch. But we also have a history of delayed improvements, perhaps delayed in future generations of crafts which may be safer. And I am concerned that the tragic loss of seven astronauts tells us that we are somewhere out on this leg of the curve and not somewhere here, you know, in the flatter portion.

It's our job to try to set policies which maintain reasonable safety, a job which we share with you. You are a very good team player. You should be. But in response to specific congressional inquiry, I think that you are free to answer those inquiries.

And I want to make this a standing congressional inquiry, if you will, that whatever the optimal budget is, as we are adjusting that budget, can you work with us to find that inflection point? I'm concerned that we have gone past that inflection point in risk where the risk has become unacceptably high.

It is always going to be inherently risky to put human beings in space. I'm a strong supporter of human space exploration. But I want to invite you to work with us to find some reasonable point in here where we are not expending exceptional resources, or unnecessarily expending resources, but we are doing everything reasonable to keep humans safe in space.

Mr. **O'KEEFE.** Sure. No, absolutely, Congressman. I'm delighted to work with you to try to find what that breakpoint is. And, again, my appreciation—slide 18 again, please—is that over the course of time, we've seen a reduction in cost of activities, there has, at the same time, been an improvement in efficiencies as well as the reduction of in-flight anomalies, technical scrubs have dropped by a lot, all of the basic factors that would drive you to conclude that, as your chart suggests, as you reduce resources, you should see an enhancement of risk. If anything, what appears to suggest here is a case where efficiencies have been attained and risk has been reduced.

So the extent there are differences of view about that over the course of this past decade of whether or not that is the contributing factor to it, we really are looking forward to trying to determine how to correct that. And if we've crossed that threshold I think you've so eloquently alluded to, we really ought to figure out exactly where we make those adjustments as necessary.

But the trends are the things that I think we need to analyze here, as well as just the basic theory, that you've advanced, which is a sound one.

Representative Wu. Well, this is why I drew it in this way, because if you have effectively reduced cost and reduced risk, you've shifted this curve to the left or to the right, up or down, or diagonally, but the curve is still here——

Mr. O'KEEFE. Yes, sir.

Representative Wu.—if you make these assumptions that such a point could be statistically determined. And I just want to invite you, as this curve shifts, as policy shifts, to help us look for this curve. You and I have been in this discussion before——

Mr. O'KEEFE. Yes, sir.

Representative Wu.—about the worthiness of human space flight. And I want to remind you of our conversation that Lewis and Clark went west 200 years ago. They got an Appropriation of $2,500. They spent $38,000, and that caused President Jefferson a lot of heartache. But that turned out to be a pretty good deal for America in the long-term.

And I would just encourage you to aggressively ask for what you need and to keep the explorers safe out there.

Senator BROWNBACK. The gentleman's time has expired.

Representative Wu. Thank you, Mr. Chairman.

Chairman BOEHLERT. Thank you, Mr. Wu.

Senator Burns.

Senator BURNS. We need you on Appropriations.

(Laughter.)

Senator **BURNS.** Mr. O'Keefe, I wish we were meeting under different circumstances, but we are not. And my question is a general question, because I was pretty close to the negotiations of the International Space Station and the agreement that we signed with Russia.

And at that time, I asked a question that we really didn't pursue for some reason or other. I think it would help this committee if— as you know, we look at programs and the infrastructure that it takes to carry those programs out. At the time we built the orbiter, was there any estimates of—what every program goes through is, there is a point diminishing returns whenever upgrades are not sufficient to carry out the mission, and I'm wondering if any estimates early on this program were made by engineers of at what point do we come to a point of diminishing returns. And if we could look at that and then—and I know programs change and missions change, and if history tells us anything, we should be looking at those kind of things in order to change the way Congress should be shouldering its responsibility.

Mr. **O'KEEFE.** Yes, sir.

Senator **BURNS.** And I would just ask if there were—any research could be done in your records of when do we reach that point, did we reach that point, and what was—and as programs change, what is being dictated in the future if this equipment is going to be asked to do things maybe it was never intended to do.

I'm not going to go over the past, because I've been intimately involved with it. And no other program stimulates the curiosity or the interest in our sciences and our mathematics in our schools like this particular agency of the United States Government. And so I deem it very, very important.

But if we could have a history and see the things that we can do, and then you do what you do best, we may have to call on our older end of the engineers, so to speak, to make those determinations, but I think it would help us a lot if we could reach back there and look at history, take a look at what happened, and then make some decisions to enable you. We don't want to see this happen again, but we know that this will happen. Accidents will happen, especially in the area of going into the unknown.

And I thank you for being here today and some explanations we've reached today. I'm looking for history, something that we base policy on into the future, upon your recommendations.

Mr. **O'KEEFE.** Well, thank you, Senator. I'd be delighted to provide that. We'll go through that consideration. There is no question that as it pertains to current flight operations, and I want to reiterate, we have a culture that is just obsessing over not letting anything go until it's all exactly right. If the investigation board found that systemically we have failed in that quest, that's precisely what we'll be guided by, as well.

But your point is very well taken. I think we've got to really be thinking seriously about where is that stage where we really make those decisions, and I think we'll provide that, for sure. I'll work through that analysis and provide it for the record, as well.

Senator **BURNS.** Thank you for your leadership, and I appreciate your cooperation.

Chairman **BOEHLERT.** The time of the Senator has expired.

Mr. **O'KEEFE.** Thank you, Senator. I appreciate it very much.

Chairman **BOEHLERT.** Thank you very much. We're going to take a brief five-minute break. Five minutes only. And then we're right back. And when we come back, Mr. Nethercutt starts the questioning.

Chairman **BOEHLERT.** The Committee will resume.

The Chair recognizes Mr. Nethercutt.

Representative **NETHERCUTT.** Thank you, Mr. Chairman.

Mr. O'Keefe, I want to welcome you, sir. Over here.

(Laughter.)

Representative **NETHERCUTT.** I know, I moved.

I appreciate your being here, and I appreciate the sensitivity with which you and the entire NASA team reacted to this terrible tragedy. I certainly was touched by Senator Stevens' remarks and agree with him with respect to your integrity and your qualifications.

Mr. **O'KEEFE.** Thank you, Congressman.

Representative **NETHERCUTT.** Thank you.

The crew that we lost touched my Eastern Washington District. Michael Anderson was a proud product of our community, and Ron Dittemore certainly is, too. And so it touched our community very deeply. But in that respect, we're respectful of all that they have done and, in the case of the NASA team, will continue to do.

This was a science-driven crew. They spent 16 days in space and were 16 minutes from landing. And in the process, with the space research double module, we're doing tremendous numbers of experiments, as I understand it. And with the loss of the *Columbia*, the question comes, what data might we have been able to collect with respect to their 16 days of scientific research efforts? And maybe that's my question, basically, is what were we able to retain and preserve with respect to their scientific research legacy?

Mr. **O'KEEFE.** Yes, sir. No question, it was an extraordinary mission. It was intensively science focused. You've characterized it exactly right. Over 16 days, a lot of the data and returns from many of those experiments were relayed back, and so the scientific community has the benefit of that information. But, to be sure, the physical laboratory as well as the physical experimentation that was aboard STS–107 is lost for all eternity. There's no question there.

But let me provide for you for the record a rundown of the kind of data and information we have gotten back, categorized by the kind of areas. But it was a phenomenal trove of information that I think will yet prove to be very enlightening information as research continues on a range of biomedical as well as physical sciences research and material research activities in the future.

Representative **NETHERCUTT.** Let me ask you if there is any support that NASA will offer to the principal investigators who lost scientific capability as well. Have you been able to assess that yet or make any judgments about the principal investigators and what losses might have been sustained as the *Columbia* was lost?

Mr. **O'KEEFE.** Yes, sir. There are a number of folks who had based a lot of experimentation, their entire dissertations were riding on this, so years of research activity has really been set back dramatically as a result of that. That's inconsequential, though, by comparison to the loss of lives, to be sure, but it is something we need to be extremely mindful of.

There was to have been a get together this past week, I think, with the biological and physical research components of our agency with all the principal investigators that had a stake, if you will, in the STS–107 experiment and research regime. We are certainly intent on trying to reconvene that session to find out what may be remedial for their efforts as we work through this, in terms of the kind of information we might look to in future flights. But we will work that. I assure you, that's something that's prominent on our minds, as well.

Representative **NETHERCUTT.** Is your commitment lessened or diminished at all to scientific research and the value of station and the efforts that were undertaken by this crew?

Mr. **O'KEEFE.** No one iota. As a matter of fact, the families of the STS–107 crew, the most stoic, courageous people you would ever want to meet, within two hours of this activity were already saying, "You know, you cannot give up on this set of objectives. They dedicated their lives to this. That's what they were committed to doing. You cannot move away from it." It had been an inspirational group, and that, in and of itself, has been sufficient cause in my mind to not step back from our commitments in this regard one inch.

I appreciate it, Congressman. Thank you.

Representative **NETHERCUTT.** Thank you.

Senator **BROWNBACK.** The time of the Member has expired.

And if I could ask the people operating the door if you could keep that door closed as much as possible, there is some beautiful singing going on outside, but we don't need it in the room.

Now, I have the only astronaut that's serving currently in the United States Senate, Senator Nelson, from Florida.

Senator **NELSON.** Thank you, Mr. Chairman.

Mr. O'Keefe, prior to you arriving at NASA, the Space Shuttle budget was whacked by some $1.4 billion. Basically, part of that over a nine-year period, this says. And, by the way, it's not the easiest to find this out, because prior to your arrival back in the early '90's, everything was lumped in together into a human space flight account—the Space Shuttle, the kinds of new technologies, plus the station. But when you break it out, what you find is that the Congress whacked part of it, about $600 million, out of the Space Shuttle, and then NASA itself whacked another $750 million.

Putting those two together, you can see the years. And this is prior to you arriving, in '02. That year, the Congress had added some $45 million, and NASA had whacked $70 million to the Space Shuttle.

So this will be an ongoing dialogue that we will have. But the question is, What is your opinion, prior to your arrival, as you look back, what had happened over that nine-year period? Sometimes the Congress would take the money out or just reduce it. Sometimes NASA would basically reprogram the money and take it out the Space Shuttle and put it elsewhere. Does that compromise safety?

Mr. **O'KEEFE.** Well, sir, I don't know the audit trail, clearly, as well as you've obviously researched this. But this particular, I think, matches with what you've projected here, which is the funding history. And the convergence of two events—and, again, I've got to really look at this in much greater detail to see the individual year changes that have occurred and so forth—but the trends seem to connote two things.

The first one is that at the same time that efficiencies were being yielded and different ways of going about business that are more risk management and more what I would call quality-assurance-related approaches that raises and improves the risk-management probabilities, at the same time also yielded some cost reductions along the way by not having an intensive group of individuals involved in the activity. And so all the indicators over this same span of time seem to suggest—but, again, we've got to back and really look at this very, very carefully—would seem to suggest that there were improvements in incidents prior to launch, incidents on orbit, all of the trend lines that we use to measure the efficiency and performance of the space flight operations program seem to be moving in that kind of a trend line.

That said, we're going to be guided by what the Gehman Board looks at as systemic causes. If this appears to have been a contributing factor, we will be right back here looking at what those fixes need to be to work on that.

Senator **NELSON.** And we will carry on a continuing dialogue on this. I can tell you, there are people at NASA and in the astronaut office that feel like that safety has been compromised over the last 10 years as a result of the Space Shuttle budget being raided. And that's something that we've got to be concerned about.

One other item——

Mr. **O'KEEFE.** We're happy to hear those comments and any other views from anybody inside to external to the agency. It'll come to ground truth and find the answers to what happened in this case, absolutely, Senator.

Senator **NELSON.** Might you comment on the fact that if that——

Senator **BROWNBACK.** I'm sorry, the time of the Senator has expired. We're having to stay on very tight time frames.

Chairman **BOEHLERT.** The Chair recognizes Mr. Weiner.

Representative **WEINER.** Thank you. Welcome.

I fear in your statement you have articulated, I guess, a strawman that some of my colleagues in their questions have knocked down. And when you said that we ought not turn our backs on exploration and that the research that was done on the Shuttle was valuable in cancer treatment, crop yield, and fire suppression, and dust storms. But it is a fact that all of that research could have, should have, and would have been done on the space station had it been completed. And, in fact, the Shuttle has, more often than not, not been a research vehicle, but a delivery vehicle supporting other platforms for science, whether it be satellites or telescopes or the space station.

One of the many things that made the *Columbia* mission noteworthy was the fact that it was a pure science mission. Apparently only 11 of the last 46 Shuttles have been able to say that. It got to be so frustrating that in the 106th Congress there was actually language put into the Appropriation bill that this Shuttle should contain more research.

You know, Shuttle astronauts, I fear to say, have become, more often than not, very high skilled, often brilliant, undeniably courageous cargo carriers. And to demonstrate this point, I don't have a graphic, but you do, and I'd ask you to put up number 20.

Under something marked "safety indicators" is a chart that said launches more than ever cargo capacity up as much as 100 percent. Cargo capacity being an indicator of safety leads me to the inescapable conclusion that having more cargo means fewer flights, means safer human beings. This should not be how we measure whether someone is safe or not, because, frankly, as we learned within, I guess, 48 hours after this horrible accident, an unmanned vehicle went up and brought cargo to the space station.

And also, on chart number 18, the same chart that has the reduction of in-flight anomalies, monthly mishap frequencies, technical scrubs, brags about the increase in lift capacity to the Space Shuttle. It seems that we're mixing the need to keep people safe, which is something that I think you have articulated several times here today, with this ever-growing notion that the Space Shuttle is the only way should develop or the only way, the only means we should use to carry cargo.

We want science to be done in space. Over and over again, we, in Congress, have been asked the question, because our colleagues put it to us, "Do you want to continue the space station funding?" We all say yes. I say yes. But we have to be careful not to confuse what the Shuttle has been as a science mission. It has been a UPS truck for Space Shuttle supplies. And I'm not sure that if you believe that increasing cargo is a way to make people safer than having a manned cargo carrier is the right way to go at all. And if you'd just address that, particularly chart number 20, if you could.

Mr. **O'KEEFE.** Sure. Thank you, sir.

Cargo, in the term you've used here, means assembly and science, both. In the last four years, many of the Space Shuttle flights, and I think you've pointed out the history precisely right, that we have dedicated the use of Shuttle for the purpose of bringing up large sections of the International Space Station for on-orbit assembly.

This is an engineering marvel we're building in space. You know, there's no other way to do this. There's no way to launch the completed International Space Station in one fell swoop or one piece, so each of it's been assembled on orbit. And by no means are these UPS truck drivers.

Representative **WEINER.** No, the question, if you'll just understand, the question is not that. It is if you can bring food, if you can bring clothing, why can't you bring Space Shuttle?

Mr. **O'KEEFE.** I'm sorry, I didn't get to the answer fast enough. I apologize.

Representative **WEINER.** I'm sorry, I'm——

Mr. **O'KEEFE.** The Progress vehicle that went up the Sunday after the accident did, in fact, contain groceries, logistics supplies, those kinds of things. That's not typically what we put aboard Shuttle. There are some of those things that are there, but mostly those are carried by those unmanned autonomous capabilities that are brought in to sustain the typical consumable requirements.

Others are put aboard Shuttle, too, like water and a few other things, but typically what is, is the cargo section includes the components, the modules of the International Space Station that couldn't get there any other way, or the science. And as we see in this particular case of the STS–107 as well as on every one of the Shuttle flights, the science experimentation going up-mass to the International Space Station to bring those scientific experiments to there, there's no other way to do that. There's no way to put them aboard autonomous unmanned vehicles at this juncture that would do anything other than provide basic logistics requirements.

So I get your point. You're exactly right. We're trying to maximize the yield of what can be, as we call it, up-mass to the International Space Station or in any other orbit pattern, but, at the same time, also minimize the risk to the individuals so that really the human involvement is minimized to the point where it's actually necessary.

Senator **BROWNBACK.** The time has expired. Thank you very much.

We now have the Senator from the host state for the Johnson Space Center, state of Texas, Senator Hutchison.

Senator **HUTCHISON.** Thank you, Mr. Chairman.

And I will just say, Mr. O'Keefe, I know how devastated you are. I've never seen a sadder face than yours in the last few weeks in all the pictures, and I think that you have handled the immediate aftermath very well, and I appreciate that.

Mr. **O'KEEFE.** Thank you, Senator.

Senator **HUTCHISON.** I also want to say I appreciate Mr. Rohrabacher's mention of the Texas residents who never expected anything like this but have been so supportive of NASA throughout East Texas looking for the debris, and consider themselves, sort of, deputies in the investigation, and I'm very proud of my home state, and especially the NASA people and the NASA family. I grew up in the area. I have known the NASA family since the announcement that NASA would come to Johnson, and have known the close-knit nature of that community. And I appreciate all of them, as well.

I want to talk about some of the experiments that have been successful and have made a difference in our lives really, from the National Science Biomedical Research Institute, which is not the old, past successes of space research, but the newer ones. They have developed portable infrared sensors to determine blood and tissue chemistry noninvasively, which could help us in intensive care units and ambulances be able to test people quickly and determine hemorrhaging or other maladies; developed a biosensor for microbes and toxins that has an application in the bioterrorism field for early detection and treatment, could be used by military searching caves in Afghanistan or by weapons inspectors; helped further development of a focused ultrasound system for hemorrhage control and for destroying unwanted tissues or tumors that could one day allow bloodless surgery.

Right there on the *Columbia*, they dealt—dealing with combustion, they created the weakest flame ever seen in a laboratory environment, about one/two-hundredth that of a match, which would be significant since soot contributes to 60,000 premature deaths each year in the United States.

My question is this. We do have a future in medical research. Your own board of scientists came back to you and said that is a future for manned space research. The question is: If the Space Shuttle is grounded for a year or six months, what would be the impact on research, or do you foresee something even further down the road for the use of the Shuttle? And, secondly, if the space station is not serviced by the Shuttle regularly for a long period of time, what would the capability be to continue the use of those microgravity conditions? Or do any of our international partners have a vehicle capable of servicing, including assembly, the station?

Mr. **O'KEEFE.** Thank you, Senator.

If I could, just on the front, associate myself with your comments about the folks from East Texas. Unbelievable support. And folks like C.G. Macklin, who is the city manager of Lufkin, Texas, Captain Paul Davis, from the Department of Public Safety down there, unbelievable people who have stepped up in a way that is just truly heroic, and we are grateful to them. They have never been associated with the NASA family, and yet here they are contributing in a way that really is remarkable, and we are eternally grateful to them for their assistance as we've moved through this very difficult time in working through the challenges there.

The impact on station, to be sure, is a real difficult circumstance, given the fact that the next flight that was due in March would have been a crew rotation for Expedition 6 to be replaced by Expedition 7. To the extent that we are able to get answers to the current challenges that are underway that the investigative board is looking to. If we can get back to flight and resume flight operations, there should be no diminution of that support to station.

To the extent that that doesn't happen and the best scenario is not realized, we do have the capability on the Soyuz flights, which is the twice-a-year rotation of the emergency egress capsule. Three cosmonauts were due to be sent up—cosmonauts and astronauts—were due to go up in April. We're looking at what that crew configuration is, consulting with our International Space Station partners to determine the best way to configure the crew to use it potentially as a rotation capability for the folks that are aboard International Space Station now. Ken Bowersox, Don Pettit, and Nikolai Budarin potentially have the opportunity to come back aboard that particular Soyuz return vehicle and send a replacement crew up. We're looking at what those options may call for.

In terms of the long-term sustainment of the International Space Station for science, there's no question, between now and June there is an ample trove of science aboard the station right now that Ken Bowersox assures me, and, more important, Don Pettit, who is the science officer, says has got him occupied every single day and won't be a limiting factor between now and the time the summer rolls around.

Beyond that, there's no question, it would end up likely be a sustaining capability, because, in pursuit of the earlier commentary we just had, and conversation, there is a—the up-mass, or the capability to be able to lift the science experimentation in the mid-deck lockers and so forth that are aboard the Shuttle typically are what bring the scientific experimentation return or rotation for the International Space Station to that laboratory condition, and that would not be feasible to do. You can't get all that aboard a resupply vehicle like Progress, which is unmanned and for logistics and basic consumables. For everything you take out of it, it's that much less sustaining capability we have for the human beings aboard, and the humans are going to be the primary focus of our intentions. So, therefore, we would see a limitation and a diminution of the science focus that would be aboard.

But, for right now, it is positively stationed today as it was yesterday and will continue through the balance of this time as the most capable laboratory condition we have, and we are maximizing the science, and that sustains for several months to come. We'll have to make adjustments beyond that, if this goes beyond that period of time.

Chairman **BOEHLERT.** The Senator's time has expired.

Mr. Etheridge.

Mr. **O'KEEFE.** Thank you, Senator. I appreciate it very much.

Chairman **BOEHLERT.** Mr. Etheridge.

Representative **ETHERIDGE.** Thank you, Mr. Chairman.

And, Mr. O'Keefe, thank you for being here. And let me also associate myself with expressing condolences to the families and others, and also with the concerns that many of my colleagues have expressed today to make sure this study is independent. I think that needs to be done for the confidence of this Congress and for the American people for the future of the program, which I strongly support and think it's important to continue.

And let me say the people of North Carolina share with you greatly, because we will celebrate the 100th anniversary of flight this year in two of the four celebrations in this country. So we have a deep commitment to space and to flight.

I was in school on Monday, right after the Saturday terrible disaster. Children were concerned, obviously, as they always are. You mentioned earlier, someone did, and I think it's appropriate to cover it, because this is a great teaching tool, not disasters, but space flight.

In the 1960's, President Kennedy said we're going to put a man on the Moon before the end of this decade. We didn't know we could do it. We didn't know how to do it. But it spawned the growth of scientists and engineers that you talked about that were getting ready to age out. Don't you think it's about time we had another grand plan and decide we're going to put a man on Mars or some great planet? That may be above your pay grade, but someone needs to say it so we get another generation of excited young people to decide they want to get involved.

I know the scientists we have in NASA, which is a very small, elite, capable group are there because they were excited. But we need a bigger core.

Very quickly, because I have one more question I want to get to you. That is, beyond that—and I hope you'll speak to that—on March of this year or last year, the independent Aerospace Safety Advisory Panel reported to you that, simply stated, the panel believed that the repeated postponement of safety upgrades, restoring aging infrastructure, and the failure to look far enough ahead to anticipate and correct shortfalls and critical skills and logistical availability will inevitably increase the risk of operating the Space Shuttle. However, since then, I understand that NASA has cancelled planned upgrade projects, shifted funding for upgrading further out in time, and has indicated that it needed to do more studies of what the upgrades should be and how they would be undertaken.

Can you tell us if that's true, and, if so, why and how that will help improve safety?

Mr. **O'KEEFE.** Yes, sir. To your first question on big goals, you bet, the approach that the President, I think, has advanced as a part of our plan that as a part of the strategic plan and all the objectives therein is to develop those enabling technologies that would then permit the establishment of those big goals to be attainable.

And the two major limitations that I think we have got to beat down and be very, very thorough in our efforts to explore the technology opportunities to conquer is the ability get anywhere in a period of time and speed that would inform the research agenda and also assure that humans, when they go, can survive the experience for the full duration of that flight.

And as it stands right now, based on our current technology, just to get to the edges of this solar system would take us 15 years. That's an unacceptable period of time it would take. And assuming that any of the scientists, the principal investigators, the research focus, are still interested by the time someone would arrive there is one of our biggest problems, because things change an awful lot in the span of a decade and a half.

So our first objective, which you see dominantly in last year's budget and this year's budget, is how to beat and how to conquer the in-space propulsion power generation requirements we have.

The second dimension of that is to look very carefully at how we can assure that humans survive the experience. And, again, the degradation we see of the five expedition crews who have been aboard International Space Station for sustained periods of four to six months or longer is typically a physiological challenge, and we've got to figure out how to conquer that, because the amount of time it would take to roundtrip to anywhere that seems to be of curiosity that would be informed by research and scientific objectives, and we've got to be sure that the folks can survive that experience.

So that and the radiation effects, all those things, an intensive amount of effort that you see in the budget proposal before you, is concentrated on trying to conquer those kinds of limitations and understand what it would take to assure a safe roundtrip activity in that regard.

As it pertains to the second point you raised of upgrades, what we have proposed in the budget amendment that came forward last November 13th of 2002 was a direct consequence of recommendations from both the General Accounting Office, the Safety Advisory Panel, all the different external groups that we have had reviewing what we do, have suggested that the longer-term Shuttle requirements, to the extent we want to sustain that capability, require that we look at modernizing and upgrading those capabilities each and every time, as we do in the Orbiter Major Modification Program. What's in the proposal for fiscal year '03 that the Congress is still deliberating on now and for the '04 program that the President just submitted a week ago is a very specific plan that would provide for those increases necessary to sustain this capability through the next decade, primarily for lift capacity of those requirements, as well as crew transfer capabilities to and from International Space Station and elsewhere. That's as maneuverable as we can make it.

Chairman **BOEHLERT.** The gentleman's time is expired.

Mr. **O'KEEFE.** I appreciate it very much.

Chairman **BOEHLERT.** Mr. Smith.

Re-evaluating NASA's Mission

Representative **SMITH.** Thank you, Mr. Chairman.

I don't have any question beyond those that have already been asked, but I do have a statement I'd like to make and then I'd welcome Mr. O'Keefe's comments when I finish.

Mr. Chairman, I have long supported our efforts to learn more about the universe around us. In fact, I've always thought that a great rallying cry would be "one percent for space." That is, we should commit one percent of our national budget, or about double what we now spend, on scientific discoveries beyond the bounds of Earth.

The *Columbia* disaster, though, has made me question not our financial commitment, but the nature of our space initiatives. Perhaps we should re-evaluate some of our missions.

Launching astronauts into an inherently dangerous environment is always risky. Such efforts should be made only when the results justify the sacrifices. That may mean NASA undertakes fewer manned missions and more unmanned ones.

From what I read and hear, astronauts on the space station spend most of their time on maintenance and conducting experiments that could be performed by mechanical means. Of course, human judgment sometimes is indispensable, so there always will be a need for manned missions. But robotics should be employed more often. They can achieve our scientific goals more cheaply and with less risk to astronauts' lives. In other words, can we justify decades of repetitious yet demonstrably lethal roundtrip Shuttle flights to a space station that has not met expectations?

It's tempting to aim farther, at an inhabited outpost on Mars, for example. However, that endeavor could be one hundred times or maybe one thousand times more dangerous than a Shuttle flight. And through the video eyes of a Martian rover, we've seen what the planet already looks like up close.

Nor are prospects great for exploring our cosmic neighborhood, considering the distances involved. Our fastest spacecraft can travel a hundred times faster than a bullet. Yet even at that incredible speed, such vehicles would take 100,000 years to reach the nearest stars.

There is a way to reach across the expansive space, seize the public's imagination, and learn more about ourselves and the cosmos, and that is to search for signs of life elsewhere in the universe. A new generation of telescopes launched into space would be able to identify life on worlds orbiting nearby stars. Other types of telescopes could detect radio or light signals from distant civilizations.

Discovering the probable existence of life "out there" would cause more excitement than any news event in the history of humankind. It would certainly be a showstopper. And the possibility of extraterrestrial life, a show-starter for our next major space program. Searching for something more than microbes, for planets like the Earth, and for other sentient life forms could lift our faces again to the heavens with hope and expectation.

Shuttle flights using new space planes would service these telescopes. No doubt, such operations will often require the good judgment and capable skills of astronauts. And astronauts who have gone before, such as those aboard the *Columbia*, will have laid a foundation from which we can push off seeking to discern the secrets of the universe.

Mr. O'Keefe, I'd like for you to respond to the idea, if not my specifics, then the general idea of reframing the mission that we have in mind. And if you have other suggestions, I'd be happy to hear them. I mentioned one for seizing that public's imagination and yet I'm learning more about the universe, and I'd be happy for you to respond to those suggestions.

Mr. **O'KEEFE.** Yes, sir. Well, no, I thank you for the very thoughtful commentary. And those are, I think, the same kind of issues we're wrestling with, in terms of what our appropriate strategy should be.

It's not an either/or proposition; it's a capability in which you build on the robotic unmanned, non-human intervention of capabilities that you can deploy and then utilize human requirements when necessary.

Again, the best example I've come across in my short one year of tenure at NASA is the Hubble Space Telescope. It is just a remarkable instrument today. It's something that is rewriting the astronomy books. Folks are just marveling at the capacity and the imagery that's coming back from the information from the Hubble Telescope is not only the new imagery that we're getting, but it's also informing the archival data that was collected in the last few years that suddenly now makes more sense because of the information we're getting today that now puts that in a different context and makes it more spectacular.

The reality is, that fantastic instrument would never have worked had we not had the capacity to launch a Space Shuttle and send folks to the Hubble Space Telescope to make the adjustments to correct the problems, which was, again, roundly considered to be space trash 10 years ago. This same instrument that was roundly, you know, dismissed as a mistake, has turned into a marvelous piece of machinery.

Representative **SMITH.** I just think we need more instruments just like that, but a bigger program and a more expensive——

I know my time is up. Maybe we can discuss this further later one.

Mr. **O'KEEFE.** Yes, sir. But I hasten to add, as well, that what you see before you in the current configuration of International Space Station is the same kind of example. This is a work in progress. We are six flights away from still achieving what is a core configuration. It had been planned to be resumed by this time next year, is where we'd be in that configuration, to build the scientific laboratories around it. But, at present, we're still looking at an amazing laboratory condition that is, in contrast to your characterization, sir, with all due respect, they are spending a lot more time on the science on these—and, matter of fact, the last two expeditions, Peggy Whitson just returned as the first science officer aboard, as we have transitioned from this engineering phase to one that's more intensively focused on the science.

It does take a lot, at least two folks to maintain it. No question about it. But it is—as we are able to build the crew capacity and focus on the scientific objectives, once we have reached a configuration that would permit that full use of the laboratory, it's going to be, I think, the same result that we saw out of Hubble in the long-term, which is going to yield the kinds of breakthroughs that we never dared imagine.

As humans, we are impatient. We want to see it now. And yet, at the same time, I think the persistence that we're trying to exert is to say, and the perseverance, is to make sure that we have that capability so that those kinds of revelations, like what we see today coming from our Hubble in our stick-to-it-iveness over this past decade yields the return we'd hope for. And it is today, and it will tomorrow, if we keep this up.

Chairman **BOEHLERT.** Thank you very much, Mr. O'Keefe.

Mr. **O'KEEFE.** Thank you, sir. I appreciate it.

Chairman **BOEHLERT.** You will note, and you're a frequent witness our panel, the House members are particularly skilled at time management, because we operate under different rules. And so they've developed the knack for asking—using all their time to ask their question, and then obviously we'll give you the opportunity to respond, because no question should go unresponded to. But we're going to stick, as much as possible, to the time limitations in the interest of all concerns.

The Chair now recognizes another skilled practitioner of the art of questioning, Ms. Jackson Lee.

Representative **JACKSON LEE.** Mr. Chairman, what an introduction.

(Laughter.)

Representative **JACKSON LEE.** Let me thank the Chairman and the Chairman of the Senate Committee for this opportunity.

And, to Mr. O'Keefe, you have shown the proudness and wisdom that we have seen over the last two weeks, compounded, of course, or matched, with your compassion and love for the NASA family. My sympathy to the extended family, and specifically to the families of the astronaut, *Columbia* seven. A local newspaper called them "Astronauts, The Heroes Next Door." And I do want to announce to you, and we're very pleased, that now almost 80 members of Congress in H.R. 525 have joined us to give them the Congressional Gold Medal, which is the highest civilian honor. And we look forward to NASA supporting us. We believe that we can move this legislation quickly. We are going to call on our Senate colleagues in that, and we are very grateful to Republicans and Democrats who have signed onto this legislation very quickly.

I think the important message that I'd like to convey in my brief time is that the Shuttle will fly again, and that the challenge should be, for lack of a better term, that it flies sooner rather than later, sooner than two-and-a-half years, sooner than three years.

You've heard this before, so let me focus on it again. I think it is extremely important that we have the Admiral's committee expanded, and I think it you need to consider the likes of a Nobel laureate, an academic, some industry engineers should be considered, some advocates of aviation. And, I believe, after 9/11, depending on their desires, family members or representatives should be considered to be part of this committee, because our job is to instill confidence in the employees, in the families, in the astronauts, not necessarily in that order, and the American people and this Congress.

And I'm reminded of the Rogers Commission that had a subsection, the Silent Safety Program. And I assume if I was to read that, it would again comment on the issue of safety.

Let me bring these points to you and tell you what I'd like to hear, whether it be in writing or you'll be able to say it now. I want actual dots, a road map, to lead me from —or to the conclusion, whether it be a conclusion that is not popular, that budgeting did not interfere with the safety of this program. I want an actual—we don't want to be presumptive, we don't want to speculate, and we don't want to be afraid of saying "mistakes."

I want to be able to understand about the frozen foam that fell under the underbelly and then hit the left leaning wing, and how we can speculate that that didn't count, when we had a report in 1994 from Stanford and Carnegie that suggested 15 percent of the tiles could count for 85 percent of the damage. And I understand an engineer in 1997, most recently, said that he thought debris falling might have an impact. And as we all know, this goes on its belly, and, therefore, it's possible for debris to hit while it was enroute or while it was in space. So I'd like the direct lines to that.

I'd like to also say that an orbiter Shuttle is excellent, but I'm very interested in payload. I think it is a valuable part of what we do, and I would not want to just have a vehicle that transported human beings, because I want research to be able to be done, because we're saving lives. And if you can comment on that idea, because I understand that we're pushing forward with the research on the orbiter, I am certainly excited about that, but I want to make sure we can carry a good payload so that that research, that vital research, can be done.

If you can comment on the fact of the icicle that fell, I call it that, and why we could suggest, or should suggest, that that was not a problem, and that you will instruct, or however the instructions are, to this commission, the committee headed by Admiral Gehman, that he will leave no stone unturned and that we'll be able to track or follow his tracks.

Budget cuts that did occur did not have an impact. An aging vehicle did or did not have an impact, 30 some years old.

Chairman **BOEHLERT.** The gentlelady's time has expired, proving the point.

Representative **JACKSON LEE.** And I thank the distinguished Chairman.

Chairman **BOEHLERT.** Mr. O'Keefe, you have.

Representative **JACKSON LEE.** I had come to an end of my sentence. If the——

Chairman **BOEHLERT.** Well, thank you very much.

Representative **JACKSON LEE.** If he——

Chairman **BOEHLERT.** Mr. Administrator——

Representative **JACKSON LEE.**—could comment briefly, I would appreciate it.

Chairman **BOEHLERT.**—you'll have the opportunity to respond, by all means. We would not——

Representative **JACKSON LEE.** Thank you very much, Mr. Chairman.

Chairman **BOEHLERT.**—cut off——

Mr. **O'KEEFE.** Thank you. Very probing questions, no question, all of which I think we should find the answers to, we must find the answers to, to understand exactly what happened to the *Columbia*. And the investigative board, when they come to conclusion on each of those points, we positively will be guided by it.

But let me offer the following observations. Everything we've seen on the budget and the resource profile for Shuttle would suggest that concurrent with improvements in efficiencies, there were also improvements in performance. And to the extent that doesn't bear out, to the extent there are systemic problems that the investigative board concludes led to this tragedy, that's the kind of thing we'll have to fix, too. And their charter is broad enough to cover that range of issues. We're not just looking for a technical finding of what happened on this one flight. Anything else they want to observe, they are free to do so, and we'll be guided by their view.

The operational problems, again, I really want to avoid any

favorite theory of what it is that could have contributed to this. We have closed off no branch in this fault-tree analysis, if you will. We want to make sure that everything is analyzed, every possible thing that could have contributed to this, to include the foam pulling off the External Tank, whatever. All of those are theories that, again, are current. They're certainly plausible, and we're going to be guided by the investigative board's conclusions of what their ultimate contribution was in these kind of cases. So I really want to be sure we're not shutting off any of those avenues, but, at the same time, not pursuing one we think is more likely or favorable or not.

In my limited experience with dealing with crisis circumstances or management of situations where you're responding to incidents, typically one of the variables that occurs, not always, but many, many times, the initial evidence proves to be not nearly as illuminating as it was when it first came out. And so rather than tracing or chasing what turns out to be a blind alley, and, therefore, foreclosing and letting the trail go cold on all kinds of other options, we're trying to maintain an even-keel approach of being sure that we not go out and favor one favored approach versus another, and to let all the evidence, let the facts speak for what ultimately occurred in this case. So we're avoiding that.

And I, too, am looking forward to the assessment of the investigative board's conclusions about how that particular item— whether it was the contributor or not. And that's what I'll be guided by as we move along.

Lastly, your observation that you asked the science content. Absolutely, we have to really maximize that. That's the—the risk that we deal with each day, those seven heroic folks who went aboard the *Columbia* were making a contribution to, ultimately, the science and research objectives. We have to have a equally intensive and disciplined approach about what we would ask them to risk their lives for, and be equally serious about it for every one of those cases in which we ask folks to venture off to do these things.

And so we've got to be as disciplined as they are in their training of assuring that the science and the research yield we think could come from this meets that same test and standard. And that's what we're about, that's what I think we're attempting to do on International Space Station. We're trying to build that capacity to yield those kinds of breakthroughs that would never be possible were it not for that facility that can't be duplicated here on Earth. So we continue in that pursuit. We are completely in agreement on that, really, imperative to be that serious about it. And I thank you for your observations.

Chairman **BOEHLERT.** Thank you very much, Mr. Administrator.

Representative **JACKSON LEE.** Thank you, Mr. Chairman.

Chairman **BOEHLERT.** Mr. Feeney.

Representative **FEENEY.** Thank you, Mr. Chairman, and for Chairman McCain and the Senate for their hospitality today.

Mr. O'Keefe, it's great to talk to you. I know it's been a very difficult weeks for you and your staff, and I would wonder if you could comment on a couple of thoughts that I had.

Number one, within about 15 minutes of the *Columbia*'s failure to land on time at Kennedy Space Center, there was a contingency plan put into place, and I'd like to know what, if any, steps you took upon assuming the control of the administration at NASA with respect to reviewing, familiarizing yourself with the contingency plan and what you found.

And, secondly, I was struck by the portion of your testimony when you spoke. I think you used the phrase "the ethos of safety at NASA," and I think you included the contractors who work for NASA, as well.

Not long ago, you and I sat as we hoped for a liftoff. We didn't get one that day. But in the audience, a young man was introduced by the name of David Strait. I wasn't familiar with his name. I thought, by the reception he got from the people there that day, he must be a rock star or a TV star. I don't watch much TV or listen to much music, either.

But I wonder if you could comment on the fact that the people involved in this program are passionate about it, what your view of their professionalism is, and what we can do as we go through this very difficult process of the investigation, the fix of the problem, and hopefully creating a new vision of space to enhance that esprit de corps during some tough times.

Mr. **O'KEEFE.** Thank you, Congressman.

The issue of the contingency plan, no question, this was something that occupied my interest from the first hour that I was privileged to be in the capacity as administrator at NASA. On the first day I walked into the office, I asked folks to please take off the shelf whatever it is, whatever that plan is, of how we would respond to a disaster like *Challenger.* And I asked that that meeting occur within an hour of when I requested it so that nobody would have to feel like they have to run off and make something up, that they'd just pull off the shelf what was there. And we sat down and reviewed that plan, and it clearly is of the origin from the *Challenger* circumstance, no question, an awful lot of the contingency planning efforts that went into it. And I reviewed it in great detail, to assure myself that I would have some working familiarity with it.

Then I asked our senior leadership folks to then benchmark it against the only other community I know of that is as equally obsessed with safety as NASA is, which is the nuclear reactors community, the naval reactors community, the legacy of Hyman Rickover and all the folks who have, over 40-plus years, have operated safely over 125 billion miles, they say, of safe operations of nuclear reactors.

So we imposed upon Admiral Skip Bowman, who is the head of naval reactors today, who is Rickover's successor several times removed now, to benchmark, help us benchmark, relative to the approach of what they use as their contingency planning efforts. Over the course of the next six months, we were able to compare notes, if you will, upgrade our plan, he upgraded his based on the way we do business, too. We both benefitted by the exercise. The contingency plan was updated and republished in September of 2002. We ran a simulation of it in November, secure in the confidence we'd never have to use it. But, nonetheless, it was organized that way.

And specifically, all the folks who were to be on the Independent Investigation Board, named, identified by position, were notified so that everybody understood the procedure. All the folks internally were exercised on the activity. And we were confident we'd never have to really worry about using something like this.

On the day it occurred, at 9:29, Bill Readdy had it with him, as did all the senior officials at Kennedy, opened up the first page, and we went to item one on that contingency plan. And it was the saddest moment I can ever recall, to be followed by the most tragic moment I've ever experienced in my life, which was to face the families of these crew members, but to tell them and to reassure them that we are working through this as diligently as we know how to find what caused this, what are the answers, how are we going to fix this, and assure that we pursue the same dream that their spouses, loved ones, fathers and mothers wanted to see pursued.

And so this plan is as good as we know how to put it together. It is that legacy. It has been really worked as smart as we know how.

And the safety ethos, if I can get to slide 23 real quick, to be sure, the example you cited, the fellow you talked about, David Strait, notice on the lefthand of this chart, there's—you can barely even see it—there's a hairline facture of no more than about an inch and a half that was enough to ground the entire orbiter fleet for four months until we knew what was the source of that problem. How did it happen? It isn't supposed to have shown up in anything. We stopped all flight operations, made the repair area to it that you see on the right over the course of that time, after they had run many, many simulations of this to figure out what the right answer was. And yet there's a bead weld right above it that was there without any consequence since the day this orbiter was first put together. And this effect was made on all four of those Shuttle flights.

So even something as minuscule as that that David Strait, with 20–20 vision, noticed as he just went through his routine business, like they all do, of inspecting the orbiter, every square inch of it after every flight, noticed that seemingly innocuous problem, and that was enough to ground that fleet for four months.

Chairman **BOEHLERT.** The gentleman's time has expired.

Ms. Lofgren.

Representative **LOFGREN.** Thank you, Mr. Chairman. I'd like to thank you, as well as Senator McCain, for convening this hearing. Over the next few months, I think all of us will be asking tough questions related to the loss of the *Columbia*, as well as the future of the space program.

But it's appropriate that first our country has paused to reflect on the heroism of the seven astronauts who gave their lives so that the dreams of humans reaching for the stars could live forever. And my thoughts and prayers are with the families of those we lost, as well as to the extended NASA family. And I know from my own experience that part of our NASA family at home, at NASA–Ames, is very much grieving with the rest of the country over this loss.

You know, I also believe that this committee is going to focus on asking difficult questions that relate to how we're best able to resume our quest to explore space, and that's really the best way to honor those who were lost, to ask those tough questions and to find answers.

Clearly, we're not going to find the answer to the specific technical issues relative to the *Columbia*. We've got technical people to do that. But it is appropriate for us to examine our own actions and to question each other about the policies and whether those policies had any impact on the risk that was inherent in this flight.

Clearly, at least into the foreseeable future, space flight will be risky. And we know that the percentage of odds right now is— although initially we thought that the use of these vehicles would have a risk of one in one-hundred-thousand, it's down to now one in fifty-seven if you just look at the records. And so we need to— I'm a believer in human space travel, but we need to make sure that we're doing our part to minimize the risks.

Now, I was late for this hearing, and I wish to apologize. It's been a big science day. We spent all morning on stem cell research in the Judiciary Committee, and I have hopes that science will do better in the Science Committee than science did in the Judiciary Committee today.

But one of the questions I have for you, Administrator, is; as we look at what we should do to make sure that the risks are minimized, were there any safety upgrade proposals ever made to you, either as Administrator or in your prior life over at the OMB, that you did not support? And if so, what were those recommendations, and why did you reach the conclusion that you did?

Mr. **O'KEEFE**. Not that I'm aware of, but I certainly will review the history of both of my capacities in the course of this Administration and ascertain the dates of when there were any deferrals or anything else of any upgrades that would be categorized as exclusively focused on safety. So, to my knowledge, we have not done so.

The only issues I'm aware of is an Electric Auxiliary Power Unit upgrade that had been planned that was determined to be technically deficient and wasn't—you know, so, in other words, no amount of money we threw at it was going to yield its performance in the manner in which it would contribute to not only efficiency but also safety characterization—that was deferred. And we're now re-examining to figure out how we can pick that up or continue it in the future that would yield the performance requirements we know of.

But we will go back, and I will submit for the record any other changes that were made during the course of— well, since Inauguration Day 2001, and if there are any changes that have occurred in that time, we'll certainly report those.

Representative **LOFGREN**. So you'll go back and review the record and take a look at your—obviously, hindsight's 20–20; we're all doing that in terms of our own activities —what you recommended both at OMB and in your role as NASA Administrator. And I know my time——

Mr. **O'KEEFE.** I'll do my best.

Representative **LOFGREN.** Thank you very much. And my time is up, Mr. Chairman. I appreciate it very much.

Chairman **BOEHLERT.** Thank you very much.

The Chair recognizes the Senator from Washington.

Lessons From the *Challenger INVESTIGATION*

Senator **CANTWELL.** Thank you, Mr. Chairman. And thank you, Mr. O'Keefe, for your diligence today. I've been to several meetings since I first checked in here this morning, and I think you've had a total of a five-minute break. So thank you for your diligence in answering these questions.

I don't think any of my colleagues have asked specifically about the lessons learned from the *Challenger* inquiry. And I don't know if, in this current configuration of the *Columbia* inquiry, you think that we have a sufficient independent scientist on this review team.

Mr. **O'KEEFE.** Yes, Senator, very specifically, the contingency review plan and the activation of an investigative board is a direct outgrowth and a direct education from the *Challenger* accident. So what we put in motion on the day of the accident was something that was a lesson learned from *Challenger.* It was part of the Rogers Commission recommendations of how we would proceed in various cases, and this is an outgrowth of one of their concerns, which is how to get ahead of these cases as quickly as possible.

The investigative board was appointed the same day as the accident. So, as a result, that was a very clear result of the lesson learned that came from that.

So an awful lot of what we attempted to do here is to build on that experience and assure that we have a result, in this case, that is driven by our interest in absolute dedication to finding the answers to what caused the terrible tragedy, find the solutions to it, the fixes, and get about the business of getting back to safe flight to support the folks aboard International Space Station.

Senator **CANTWELL.** So who is that independent scientist, then, on——

Mr. **O'KEEFE.** Oh, I'm sorry. The independent—there is—I spoke as recently as last night to Admiral Hal Gehman, who is the chairman of the current board, who has five different folks he has in mind, I'm told, who are physicists, scientists, etcetera, that he is considering to propose for addition on the board. I have advised him whoever he wants to put on that board that will expand his expertise, that will improve the independence of the board, help its objectivity, we will do it without qualification and without hesitation.

Senator **CANTWELL.** Well, I am struck, reading last night and this morning, the Feynman minority report to that report that I think finally got in as an appendix in which Mr. Feynman was very critical of discrepancies between engineers and managers as the probability of failure. So you had engineers having studies and analysis saying that maybe the risk is a lot higher than what the high-level managers thought. The criteria used for flight-readiness reviews often developed a gradual decreasing strictness, "If the Shuttle had flown with it before, chances are it worked before, so let's just—let's not think about the variations that might happen."

The Feynman Report even said NASA might have exaggerated the reliability of product, that there were variations in models, that NASA was more of a top-down system in testing the entire system instead of testing the individual properties and limitations of the material within the Shuttle to the degree that I think the report was quite critical of NASA, in the sense of maybe even coming to Congress and catering to us in the public relations expectations that were there by the public, instead of relying back on this basic engineering information.

So I guess my concern is, is that the panel, as I see it now, doesn't have that Feynman voice, and I think what we really do want to do here is make sure that we are not engaged in that PR battle, but understanding how we really do build the NASA systems of the future——

Mr. **O'KEEFE.** Right.

Senator **CANTWELL.**—with more reliability and predictability based on those materials.

And so I'd be very interested in how those recommendations were actually implemented, because I have a feeling we might find the same circumstances are true here. We're going to find out that there is some material property limitations that were discovered in some report written by some engineer that somewhere along the way got translated into "not as big a risk" and, thereby, the disaster that we've all been dealing with. So I appreciate your attention.

Mr. **O'KEEFE.** Well, thank you, Senator.

That may be. And if the investigative board comes back and points to the systemic problems that we have, we positively will take that as a firm recommendation and go fix it.

What I can advise, though, in my one year experience, with no prior experience with NASA at all—this is my first year at it—and reading the *Challenger,* the Rogers Commission Report, I was a Senate Appropriations Committee staff member on the day *Challenger* blew up, read the report thereafter, and that's my only association with that up until a year ago, is—what I see is a different agency than what existed 17 years ago, in that sense.

One of the observations they made, Feynman's view, I think, was exactly right, he pointed to the difficulty of that chain of command and how it gets altered. This whole process I've witnessed, and I'm advised I'm the first Administrator to have attended what is called a Flight Readiness Review two weeks before a launch, it resembles a room like this, with everyone that you could possibly imagine associated with this activity, all of which are empowered to raise their hand during the course of a full day, sometimes two-day, review of every single technical issue. And if they disagree with the way it was presented, they disagree with the conclusion, they immediately raised their hand, and the issue was then put to the side to go work the conclusion of it. That didn't exist prior to *Challenger*. It was all done by telephonic tag-up occasionally. This is a in-the-room, everybody there associated with the activity.

There was a big difference at that time, where schedule drove everything. They were looking to get to a flight rate of 20, 30 flights a year. We're operating on a five- to six-flight-a-year approach.

And as we discussed with Congressman Feeney a minute ago, and I appreciate your bringing this out, we stopped flight operations for four months over a hairline fracture found on not the orbiter that was scheduled to go up, but one that's in an Orbiter Processing Facility. Everything ended. The engineer, the inspector, that noticed that, that stopped operations cold for four solid months.

The disjointed chain of command, that doesn't—I don't see it. We have astronauts, former astronauts, who are in capacities as high as the Deputy Administrator, the Associate Administrator for Space Flight, the Associate Administrator for Safety and Mission Assurance, all three are former astronauts. That didn't exist prior to

Challenger. None of those positions included anybody with that kind of background.

And all the way through this process, every single one of those managers are empowered, are expected, there's a responsibility that each of them feel they have, to stand up and be counted and stop all the operations until there is any issue that has been left unresolved, beaten to ground truth.

So what I've seen—and, again, from an objective opinion, I think, until a year ago, and now I'm steeped in it, there's no doubt about it—but until that time, unfamiliar with it other than what I read in the *Challenger* Rogers Commission Report, as well— would tell me this is a different place than it was then.

All that said, we will be guided by what the Gehman Board comes back and tells us was the problem here. And if it was a systemic problem, we're going to fix it. If it was a technical problem, we're going to fix that, too. There is nothing I can imagine that's not on the table, and I have no bias against any finding they could possibly come up with that wouldn't otherwise contribute to the solution in this particular case. We are going to act on that without reservation.

Chairman **BOEHLERT.** Thank you very much.

Senator **CANTWELL.** Thank you, Mr. Chairman.

Chairman **BOEHLERT.** Mr. Moore.

Representative **MOORE.** Thank you, Mr. Chairman. Thank you, Mr. O'Keefe, for staying.

Yesterday, in the *Washington Post,* it was reported, I believe, that you said that—you defended the way you set up the accident investigation board, arguing that you proceeded the way you did so that it could launch an investigation immediately with members who were already well briefed on Shuttle operations. I guess my question is, Mr. O'Keefe, how important it is that we launch an investigation immediately, or should we take a more slow and diligent approach, as I think you said to Ms. Sheila Jackson Lee recently? I'm just—I'm asking what kind of investigation do we need here? What's, in your opinion, the best approach?

Mr. **O'KEEFE.** Yes, sir, thank you.

I believe what I tried to say—and if I was inarticulate, I apologize—was to say we developed a contingency plan to activate an investigative board so that they could act immediately, get on with the task immediately. They are not—and if I said this, I am in error, and I need to correct the record—they are not conversant in Shuttle operations.

There is only one member of the group who is even vaguely familiar with NASA operations. The rest of them have had no experience with NASA at all. The chairman of board is Hal Gehman, a United States Navy admiral, retired, who never had any association with NASA. I don't even think he ever attended a launch before. All of the other members of the board are from the FAA, the Department of Transportation, the United States Navy, the United States Air Force, all folks dealing with safety, mission assurance, flight certification, etcetera. I don't know if any of them have even toured a NASA facility. They spent the past week in Shreveport, Louisiana, and have now, just now, this past Friday, arrived at Johnson Space Center, and went through the simulation of what a re-entry is like, astronaut simulations they do. None of them have ever been through that before.

So Admiral Gehman has advised me that part of what he's done this past week is get up to speed on what he calls "Shuttle 101," just to understand what the lingo means and what the acronyms are. They are, nonetheless, were available up and running and talking to each other as early as seven-and-a-half hours after the accident. On Saturday afternoon, at 5 p.m., they were already identified and ready to go.

So at least we picked up the time that gave them the opportunity to then become more familiar with the processes, the evidence, the facts, the data, so that they could get about the business of investigating as quickly as possible before the trails go cold.

That's the approach that—you know, certainly, there's no one-size-fits-all approach to this, but it certainly was one of the most effective ways to get moving.

Slide 33, if you would, at least this is what happened two days after the event. That's the folks that got there, and they're talking to FEMA, you know, managers on site, you know, it at least gave us an opportunity to get moving, as opposed to sitting around thinking about who should we pick, when should they go.

Representative **MOORE.** In terms of a realistic time frame, then, what might Congress and the American people expect us to—when you see this investigation really getting underway, and I know you can't predict what results we're going to find. I assume you can't predict what results we're going to find. But what time frame are we looking at, Mr. O'Keefe?

Mr. **O'KEEFE.** Well, the guys that's right on the other side of the fellow with the FEMA jacket on, right ahead of him, is Admiral Hal Gehman, and he can answer that question better than I can.

Representative **MOORE.** All right.

Mr. **O'KEEFE.** I wouldn't even presume to suggest when he's going to finish. And he has—there's no amount of time that's necessary that we think is appropriate to go out and find out what happened here. We're going to be guided by he and his board's view of exactly what occurred, and there is no time limit on that.

Representative **MOORE.** Very well, thank you.

Mr. **O'KEEFE.** Thank you. I appreciate it very much.

Chairman **BOEHLERT.** Thank you very much, Mr. Moore.

Mr. Administrator, I want to thank you very much. Before we wrap up, I just want to touch on a couple of more points. I want to bring clarity to a very important issue.

I think it should be self evident that the Congress is committed to the proposition, on a bipartisan, bicameral basis, that we need to strengthen the evidence supporting the assertion that the *Columbia* Accident Investigation Board is truly independent. Now, I know the message has been sent, and I think it's been received, and I know it's been heard, and I want some assurance that it will be heeded. So I'd like you to visit that a little bit more and comment.

I carefully listened to you as you said you'll consult with Admiral Gehman, but I hope you're hearing what Congress is saying. We are the ones, and others, too, insisting that we get some clarity to this issue. So can you address that a little bit more for me?

Mr. **O'KEEFE.** Yes, sir. No, I appreciate your patience on it, and I do not mean to equivocate in any way, shape, or form.

I share exactly the same objective, I think, as all Members here do, which is to determine what are the answers to this tragedy, what are the facts that led to it, and ultimately find out how we go about fixing it and getting back to safe flight.

And in that pursuit, I will not just consult with Admiral

Gehman, I will advise. As soon as this hearing is concluded, I will give him a call back and say my clear understanding from the Members of this Joint Committee is that there are aspects of the charter that need further revision. Let's examine what those might be. And, to his satisfaction, we will make a change——

Chairman **BOEHLERT.** Well, let me give you an easy one right off the bat. I mean, number 10, provide a final written report to the NASA Administrator not later than 60 days. First of all, the 60-day time frame——

Mr. **O'KEEFE.** Sure.

Chairman **BOEHLERT.**—is totally unrealistic. But the report will come to the President, to the Congress, to the American people, and to the NASA administrator simultaneously.

Mr. **O'KEEFE.** Yes, sir.

Chairman **BOEHLERT.** All right.

Mr. **O'KEEFE.** I'll make that an alteration and suggest to him that that's exactly—and we'll go ahead and make that charter change, because, again, I've stated that.

There's a letter, too, that I—that's part of the record, as well—on the 60-day issue, that, when I commissioned the panel in the very first place, said, "Our contingency plan contemplated 60 days, but you take whatever time you think you need, Mr. Chairman, Admiral, to come to conclusion on this." I'll reiterate that. We will eviscerate the 60-day. It has no bearing. It was intended as part of the continency plan originally, but not envisioned to be used. So to the extent that there is any amount of time he needs, that's what he's got. I don't intend to impose anything different on him.

Chairman **BOEHLERT.** Well, that's the easiest one.

Mr. **O'KEEFE.** Sure.

Chairman **BOEHLERT.** We have, you know, some others that——

Mr. **O'KEEFE.** Well, actually, we'll revise whatever is necessary.

Chairman **BOEHLERT.** We want to deal with it clearly so that it's clear in our own minds that they're truly independent.

Mr. **O'KEEFE.** Yes, sir.

Chairman **BOEHLERT.** And if they decide they want to go down a certain path or they want to hire a certain expert, they don't have to march over to NASA headquarters to get approval.

Mr. **O'KEEFE.** Yes, sir.

Chairman **BOEHLERT.** The admiral and the *Columbia* Accident Investigation Board have the authority to proceed as they deem best——

Mr. **O'KEEFE.** Yes, sir.

Chairman **BOEHLERT.**—to get us the answers we are all demanding. And that's critically important.

Mr. **O'KEEFE.** Yes, sir, I concur. I appreciate it. Thank you.

Chairman **BOEHLERT.** Well, I think, as we come to the end, we've done several things today. First and foremost, the current status report. And obviously, this is a very dynamic situation, so events almost change hour by hour, let alone day by day. And so that was very important.

And we've started what I have characterized in my opening remarks as the national conversation, which we have to start, people talking to each other, not through each other, over each, around each other—directly.

We have affirmed the commitment to the concept of an independent board, and we've had agreement on the need for charter changes. I think that is very important.

Now, this is not the beginning of the end; it's the end of the beginning. And we always want instant analysis of immediate findings, and that's understandable. But experience tells us we learn the most from in-depth examination of more complete data.

So now we are in the fact-assembling phase, and all of us with responsibility in this very important assignment—the Congress, NASA, the *Columbia* Accident Investigation Board—are all going about the business of assembling the facts. Then all of us will have this database to look at and take care and caution as we go forward with our special responsibilities.

Obviously, NASA and the Accident Investigation Board will be focusing more on the technical aspects. Obviously, there's a need on the part of the Congress to focus more on policy as we chart the course for the future. That does not mean they are mutually exclusive. We'll be looking at each other.

I have been very pleased with the response I've had from Admiral Gehman in assuring us that Congress will be very much involved in all of the proceedings. I have been very pleased with the cooperation we've received from Administrator O'Keefe and his team. And I have been just impressed beyond any ability to adequately explain at the total commitment I find on the part of every single person involved in this procedure to get the facts. And let us be guided by the facts as we fulfill our important responsibilities.

Mr. Administrator, thank you.

The hearing is closed.

Made in the USA
Monee, IL
09 March 2021